STAGECOACH SHOWDOWN

Slocum nearly lost his hold on the Colt as he grabbed for the doorframe to keep himself from losing his balance. The stage slowed, tipped back to an upright position and stopped.

He shoved the door open and found himself staring into the muzzle of a double-barreled shotgun. Its barrels had been sawed off short, and it was about the ugliest gun he'd ever seen.

"Stay right there, cowboy. Keep them hands up."

The man was dressed like an ordinary cowhand, and had made no attempt to cover his face. Slocum hoped it didn't mean the bandits meant to kill them all. . . .

OTHER BOOKS BY JAKE LOGAN

JAKE LOGAN

SLOCUM AND THE STAGECOACH BANDITS

BERKLEY BOOKS, NEW YORK

SLOCUM AND THE STAGECOACH BANDITS

A Berkley Book / published by arrangement with
the author

PRINTING HISTORY
Berkley edition / August 1991

ISBN: 0-425-12855-5

10 9 8 7 6 5 4 3 2 1

SLOCUM AND THE STAGECOACH BANDITS

1

John Slocum leaned back in the seat and let his head rest against the side of the stagecoach. The ride was bumpy, and the creak of the springs was driving him crazy. If he could shut out the chatter of the three people in the coach with him, he hoped the ride might go more quickly.

The heat was oppressive. He could look out through the window, but there wasn't much to see. The flat wasteland stretched to a purple haze far to the south, where Mexico loomed on the edge of the world. Between the creaking wheels and Mexico there was nothing but dry earth and cactus.

One of the two men in the stage with him was a rancher, the other an accountant and their endless conversation ran the gamut from cattle to cows. The man next to him, at least, kept his voice to a conversational level. But the man across from him seemed to shout everything around a cigar, as if his colleague were on the other side of Arizona. Every bellowed phrase was accompanied by a blue-gray cloud of smoke that hung in the still air until the fat man waved it aside with a fistful of chubby fingers. The gaudy ring on his pinky looked like it was worth more than Slocum owned. Now and then it would catch the brilliant sunlight pouring through the window and it would look as if his hand had caught fire.

The other man, who was probably half the fat man's age, seemed pleasant enough. But Slocum judged a man by the company he kept. The young rancher was either too accommodating by half or likely to end up a carbon copy of the fat man someday. By design.

The woman was another matter. If he hadn't seen her in their company, Slocum would have thought she was as much a stranger to them as he was. She stared out her own window, now and then reaching up to adjust the wide-brimmed hat that could not tame the tangle of red curls it struggled to contain.

Watching her out of the corner of his eye, he noticed a striking similarity between the woman and the younger man. It was as if God had tried something in putting the young man together, then decided it worked better on a woman and tried again. The second time, He got it right. On the young man, the features looked soft, out of place somehow, ill-suited to the hardness of Arizona.

On the woman, they were perfect. Freckles, just a few, dusted her nose and cheeks. The nose itself was delicate, with a slight tilt. Her eyes were an emerald green, but bigger than any imaginable gem. Her lips were soft; a quiet red, and fixed in a permanent pout that did not make her look ill-humored so much as thoughtful. The folds of her dress did nothing to conceal her generous figure. Her hands, placid in her lap, were strong, showed that she was not afraid to use them, yet seemed delicate.

She seemed conscious of Slocum's gaze. Her eyes caught his once and held them for a moment. Then, her lips bowing faintly into a smile, she turned back to the window.

"Where you from, cowboy?"

At first, Slocum didn't realize the words had been addressed to him. When it dawned on him that there was no one else to whom they could apply, he said, "Sorry?"

"I asked where you was from." It was the fat accountant. He let his hand hang on the window ledge now, the cigar jutting out into the desert air and trailing a thin strand of bluish smoke. He smiled, and it was not unpleasant.

Slocum shrugged. "Here and there."

The fat man smiled again. "I been both places," he said. "There's better. Got to be. Anyplace is better than here." He slapped his knee with a thick hand. He looked to the younger man for confirmation. "Ain't that right, Will?"

"Ralph, maybe the man doesn't want to talk. He looks like he's trying to rest." It was the woman. Her voice was soft, on the husky side. She smiled at Slocum. "Don't pay him any mind. Ralph just doesn't know the difference between breathing and talking. He thinks he'll die unless he talks a blue streak."

"Now, Maggie, you hush up. Let the cowboy talk for himself." Ralph patted her knee. "Talkin' helps pass the time. And God knows, we got lots of that."

Slocum nodded at Maggie. "It's all right," he said. "I'm not much of a talker, but I'm as sociable as the next man, I guess."

Maggie laughed. "Sociable doesn't have a chance when Ralph gets going."

"Where you folks headed?" Slocum asked.

Ralph started to answer, but Maggie beat him to it. "Prescott."

"Will here, got a big spread up there," Ralph said. "Was down to Yuma to talk to Colonel Martin. Wants to sell some beef to the army."

"Any luck?"

"It don't take luck, Mr.—"

"Slocum. John Slocum."

"It don't take luck, Mr. Slocum. What it takes is connections. Those he ain't got. But I'm workin' on it for him. And tryin' to teach young Will, here, how to push a little. Otherwise, he won't have much of a future in the cattle business. I'm a numbers man. I know about things like that."

"Will'll do just fine, Ralph," Maggie said.

"Long as you stay with him, Maggie. Long as you stay with him."

"He's my brother, Ralph. I'll always be with him."

"Not if you go back East, like you been talkin' about doin', almost since the first day you got out here. Since I met you, anyhow." Leaning toward Slocum, he said, "Maggie's used to the finer things. They come down on horseback, but she wanted to ride back to Prescott in style."

She looked at the interior of the stage with distaste, then at Slocum, and wrinkled her nose. "Some style," she muttered. Then, to Winslow, she said, "Mr. Slocum doesn't care about our family histories, Ralph. Why don't we all just shut up and let him rest."

"No, you go ahead, Miss—"

She smiled in embarrassment. "I'm sorry, I should have introduced myself." Then glancing at her two companions, she added, "All of us. Seems like Arizona sucks the manners out of folks, as well as the life."

"Aw, Maggie, you know—"

"Hush up, Ralph. My name is Margaret Callahan." Slocum took the extended hand. He realized he had been right about its strength, but it was far softer than he had imagined. "This is my brother, William," she continued. "And this talkative bear of a man is Ralph Winslow."

Slocum shook Winslow's hand, then Will's. "Pleased to meet you," he said.

"I just hope you can say that by the time we get to Prescott, Mr. Slocum," Maggie said, her face breaking into a radiant smile. "And unless Ralph bites his tongue, I don't think that's too likely. Of course, I could shoot him."

"Damn it, Maggie, I don't talk all that much." He stuck a thick finger under his collar. His face was red, and he looked like he'd just been caught with his hand in the cookie jar.

Maggie laughed. "Then shush!" She turned to Slocum. "What do you do, Mr. Slocum?"

"A little of everything, not much of anything. Mostly I work, except when I don't. Then I look for work. That's work, too, I guess."

"Southerner, are you?"

"Yes, ma'am. Georgia. But that was a long time ago. Forever ago, really."

"I know what you mean. I feel that way about St. Louis."

"That where you're from?"

"Boston, actually. But it's where I live now."

Winslow couldn't restrain himself. "St. Louis is where she *used* to live. She lives in Prescott, now. She just won't admit it yet."

Slocum was about to answer when the stage lurched violently. He heard the driver shout to the team, and the crack of the whip. The stage started to move faster now, and he looked at Maggie, who seemed suddenly confused.

"What's happening?" she asked.

Ralph, for a change, had nothing to say. Will Callahan leaned toward his window, stuck his head out, but drew it back quickly. "I don't see anything," he said.

Slocum wasn't satisfied. He looked out his own window. The stage was rocking now, its ancient springs creaking wildly, like old trees in a high wind. He looked behind, toward Yuma, but saw only the cloud of dust kicked up by the stage and the three horses tethered behind it. He shouted up to the driver, but got no answer.

They were rushing headlong, almost as if there was no one in charge up in the driver's seat. Swinging the door open, Slocum braced himself against the open doorframe and climbed out, leaving his feet on the floor of the passenger compartment. He shouted again.

"What the hell's going on?"

This time, someone heard him. The shotgun rider turned his head, saw Slocum, and leaned toward him. "Riders comin'."

"Trouble?"

"Could be. You'd best git back inside, mister."

"What kind of trouble?"

"Don't know. Could be nothin'. Could be Apaches. Could be just about anything. Better git back inside and stay there. We'll handle it."

Slocum shook his head. "All right. You need any help, you better give us a little warning. Maybe you should pull up."

He heard the driver say something and the shotgun rider turned away for a few seconds, then turned back. "Jake don't stop for nothing. He says to mind your own business and git inside."

Reluctantly, Slocum swung back into the passenger compartment. The fat man watched him nervously. When Slocum said, "Riders coming hard," Winslow didn't look happy.

"What riders? Who?" Will asked.

Slocum shook his head. "Don't know. Maybe nothing to worry about."

"Apaches, that's what it is. Bloodthirsty savages, they—"

"Shut up, Ralph," Will Callahan barked. Then, turning to his sister, he said, "It's probably nothing. But it doesn't hurt to be careful."

Maggie looked at Slocum. She seemed somehow less unnerved than her two companions. Slocum pulled his Colt Navy pistol and cracked it open. It was fully loaded, and he spun the cylinder to make sure everything was in working order.

"You worried, Mr. Slocum?" Maggie asked. Her voice was calm, if anything just a tad huskier than it had been. Maybe nerves, Slocum thought. And maybe not.

"Not nervous, no. But it doesn't hurt to expect the worst, ma'am. In my experience, it happens as often as not."

"Please, Mr. Slocum. You'll just upset her," Will said.

"The lady asked."

Will nodded. "Sorry, I just don't want her to worry needlessly."

The stage continued its headlong rush. Slocum listened to the springs and the crack of the whip as the driver drove his team flat out. He leaned out the window again. This time, off to the right, he spotted a cloud of dust. The riders were too far away for him to see clearly, but he knew they weren't Apaches. And there was no doubt in his mind they were chasing the stage.

Ahead, he could see a narrow notch between two sloping hills. The road wound through it, flanked by ranks of saguaro marching up either slope, then two sheer walls rose almost straight up as the notch narrowed still further.

He was just pulling back when he heard the first gunshot.

2

Slocum still didn't know whether the shot had been aimed at them or had simply been some kind of warning. The stage was drawing closer to the notch. If they could get through it, they might have a chance. At least, that's what the driver seemed to be thinking. The riders were closer now, close enough for Slocum to see there were only two of them. It didn't seem likely they were trying to rob the stage. Firing at such long range would have been nothing more than an alert that trouble was coming.

As the riders drew closer, the stage entered the notch. The ground sloped up and away from him on his side of the stage. He had the Colt in his hand, and Will Callahan was leaning out the opposite window. He also held a pistol. Ralph was doing his best to reassure Maggie, but from the muttering, Slocum realized the fat man was trying to calm himself down and using Maggie as a sounding board.

The stage careened into the mouth of the vertical walls. Suddenly, it lurched to one side. The wheels locked and spewed clouds of dust. The brakes squealed and the stage leaned dangerously, raising the wheels on the opposite side off the ground. The saddled mounts behind it whinnied in fear. Slocum was worried about his chestnut.

Slocum nearly lost his hold on the Colt as he grabbed for the doorframe to keep himself from losing his balance. The stage slowed, tipped back to an upright position, and stopped.

He reached for the door handle when he heard two quick gunshots. He shoved the door open, and found himself staring into the muzzle of a double-barreled shotgun. Its barrels had been sawed off short, and it was about the ugliest gun he'd ever seen. Slocum stopped in the doorway.

"Stay right there, cowboy." It was the man with the shotgun. He backed away a couple of steps and waved the muzzle, indicating Slocum should step on out of the coach. "Keep them hands up, buddy."

Slocum looked at the man closely. He was dressed like an ordinary cowhand, and had made no attempt to cover his face. That could mean almost anything. Slocum hoped it didn't mean the bandits meant to kill them all.

"Let's have your gun, cowboy." The shotgun-wielding man backed away another step. "Just drop it right there on the ground."

Slocum saw two more men out of the corner of his eye. They were both armed with rifles, and had them trained on the driver and shotgun rider. Behind him, Slocum could hear the approaching riders. He knew now they were part of the team. He held out the Colt, and kept one hand in the air as he did so.

"Easy, now," the gunman said. "Just use your fingertips and let it drop."

Slocum did as he was told. He looked to the rear of the stage for a moment. The chestnut seemed uninjured, but looked terrified.

"All right," the gunman shouted, "everybody else get on out of there. You got a gun, it better not be in your hand." He nodded toward his left, signaling for Slocum to move aside.

Will Callahan appeared in the doorway. He climbed down slowly, and the gunman barked, "Get a move on, sport. I ain't got all day."

Will turned back to reach into the coach and helped Maggie to the ground. Ralph Winslow came last. His pudgy face looked pale, and beads of sweat glistened on his pasty forehead.

"Well, looka here, a lady—well, well, well." He bowed at the waist in mock decorum. "How do, ma'am—" But he never took his eyes off Slocum, as if he sensed that the only threat might come from the silent Southerner.

The two riders reined in and dismounted, then sprinted toward the front of the wagon. One of them shouted, "You get the box yet?"

The man with the shotgun shook his head. "Ain't had time. Besides, you fellows got to earn your share. I figured you'd climb up and get it." He laughed, and the two newcomers glared at him.

One of them swaggered toward the front of the coach. "Let's have that strongbox," he said.

"What strongbox?"

"Don't play games, Pop. I know you got it. And I know what's in it. We didn't come out here for a country picnic. Now let's have it."

"I ain't got a strongbox."

Slocum was getting tense. He didn't know whether the driver was telling the truth, but he knew the bandit didn't believe him, and wouldn't believe him, whether he was telling the truth or not. He inched toward the man with the shotgun, who was watching the argument.

As if sensing the movement, the gunman whirled suddenly. He smiled at Slocum, then shook his head. "You don't want me to use this," he said, waving the shotgun a few inches. "Believe me, cowboy, you don't want that."

Slocum shook his head. "No, I don't want that." He knew what a load of shot would do. It would cut him in half, and maybe kill the other passengers as well.

"I want that box, Pop."

The driver held his ground. The shotgun rider reached up to take off his hat. He wiped his forehead with his sleeve. He said something Slocum didn't catch.

The outlaw was losing patience, which seemed to be in short supply to begin with. "Tell you what, Pop," he said, "I can climb up there and get it myself. But if I do that, I'm gonna kill you. If it's there, I'll be mad you lied to me. If it ain't there, I'll just plain be mad. Now, you got one chance to save your scrawny hide, and that's to give me the box. Now."

The driver sighed. "All right," he said. He reached under the seat, and Slocum heard something scrape on the wood. The driver grunted, then stood, hauling a heavy box out into the open. He tossed it off the coach and it landed with a dull thud on the sand and gravel.

"I thought you didn't have a box," the outlaw said. "I told you, don't make me mad." He pulled his pistol and walked close to the stage. "Get on down out of there," he said.

The shotgun rider stared at him blankly.

"Yeah, you. Get on down from there."

The guard shook his head and got to his feet, then turned his back to negotiate the descent. When he was on the ground, he turned back to the outlaw.

"Now you," the gunman said to the driver.

"I might as well stay right here," the driver said.

"Suit yourself."

The gunshot was louder than it should have been, maybe because no one expected it. The bullet caught the driver in the forehead, and he fell back against the seat.

"I told him not to make me mad."

Will Callahan made a move, but Slocum grabbed at his arm. Callahan shook him loose. "You murdering bastard," he shouted, lunging toward the gunman.

Slocum tried to grab him again, but too late. The outlaw turned to face him, then lashed out with the barrel of his pistol. The sharp crack of metal on bone sounded almost as loud as the gunshot.

Callahan lay on the ground, his hands cupped over his head. The gunman stepped closer and pointed his pistol straight down. "Lot of sand, this one has," he said, shaking his head. He squeezed the trigger.

Maggie screamed and rushed forward. Slocum grabbed her, looping an arm around her waist. She struggled to break free, but Slocum held on. The gunman walked away and kicked at the strongbox. He fired twice more, shattering the lock, then kicked at the ruined hardware.

"Get the stuff out of there," he said.

Two of the bandits jumped to rip the lid off the box. Slocum spotted two canvas satchels inside, both stamped U.S. Army. He glanced at the gunman, who happened to look toward him at the same moment. The gunman smiled.

Maggie took the opportunity to break from Slocum's grasp. She rushed to kneel beside Will Callahan. The back of his jacket was soaked in blood. He hadn't moved, and hadn't uttered a sound since the gunshot. Slocum knew the young man was dead, but Maggie either didn't know or refused to accept it.

She tried to turn her brother on his back, but Ralph Winslow stopped her. "You don't want to do that, Maggie. Trust me."

"If I trusted you a little less, this wouldn't have happened. Will trusted you too much. And—" She looked at Slocum then, her eyes narrow, her lips drawn to a thin white line.

"And you," she snapped, "are you going to let them get away with this?"

Slocum started to answer, but knowing there was nothing he could say that would make a difference, he hesitated, and the leader of the bandits answered for him. "There ain't nothing he can do about it, little lady. He knows that. And you best believe it. Unless you want to see him killed just as dead as them two." He waved a hand in an arc broad enough to take in her brother and the driver still in the seat of the coach.

He took a step or two and stood looking down at her. "Fact is, 'little lady' might just be an insult." He stuck a hand into the bodice of her dress and pulled it open. "No, sir, you ain't no *little* lady at all, are you, darlin'?"

She slapped his hand away, but he didn't let go, and the bodice ripped at the same moment Slocum made his move. He caught the gunman in the small of the back with his shoulder.

Slocum felt the satisfying jar of collarbone on spine, and heard the whoosh of air as the impact drove breath from the gunman's lungs. Slocum's drive carried him forward and he pulled the gunman down, landing on top of him with his full weight.

The gunman cursed and tried to turn over, wriggling to get out from under Slocum at the same time. But Slocum was too strong for him. He locked an arm around the gunman's neck and jerked his head back. The man with the shotgun sprinted over and swung the sawed-off Remington like a club, catching Slocum on the shoulder and then grabbing him around the neck.

"Do something, Ralph!" Maggie screamed. "They'll kill him."

But Ralph merely grabbed Maggie around the waist and pulled her toward the back of the stage. Slocum rolled over on his side, the pain stabbing down through his shoulder like a blade white hot from the forge. He tried to get up and narrowly avoided a second swipe from the shotgun.

Then, realizing the superior firepower it represented, the gunman turned the gun around and shoved the muzzle into Slocum's chest. "Don't make me pull the trigger, cowboy," he said. "Just don't."

"Go on, Pete. Shoot the son of a bitch," the killer said.

The one called Pete shook his head. "Been enough shooting," he said. "You shouldn't have killed them fellas, Doak."

"The hell you talkin' about? Bastard lied to me, and that other one, he just—"

"Shut up, Doak. Just shut your mouth. You caused enough trouble already. There wasn't supposed to be no killing. I told you that a hundred times."

"You was wrong, Pete, wasn't you?" Doak leered.

Slocum tried to get up. Doak saw him and swung his gun around, but Pete stepped into the line of fire, took another step, and brushed the pistol aside. "I'll handle this," he said. He backed away two steps and turned, swinging from the heels. Slocum saw the blow coming, and brought up one hand to ward it off, but it crashed into the side of his head and everything went black.

3

Slocum felt the pressure on his face. He wasn't sure what it was, and tried to push it away. Then he felt something wet trickle down over his cheeks. He wiped at it with his fingers. Slowly, his vision cleared. He saw Ralph Winslow leaning over him, rubbing at his face and pouring water from a canteen.

The fat man saw Slocum's eyelids flicker. "He's coming around, I think," he said.

Trying to sit up, Slocum ran into a wall of pain. His head throbbed, and his shoulder felt as if someone had tried to rip it off. He groaned, trying to ignore the pain and pushing himself up on his elbows.

"You all right, Slocum?"

"What happened?"

"They killed Will and the driver. You remember? Bandits. They got Maggie. The bastards, they took her with them."

"What?"

"Maggie, they took her. Doak, the one killed Will and the driver, he done it."

Slocum tried to sit all the way up. His vision was still blurry. The fat man's face swam in and out of focus. Sweat trickled down alongside his nose, making it seem as if they were both underwater. "Help me up," he said.

"You best stay right where you're at, Slocum. They like to busted your head open."

Slocum felt for the side of his head, then snapped his fingers away when they found a lump the size of an egg over his ear. The touch of his fingers sent a stab of pain so deep inside him it made him shiver.

He got up on one knee. The fat man, realizing he wasn't going to stay put, stood up, then reached down to grab him by the arms and haul Slocum to his feet.

"Which way did they go?" Slocum asked. He looked around on the ground. The shotgun rider realized what he was looking for. He handed Slocum the Colt. It was empty, and Slocum cracked it open, loaded it, and jammed it into his holster.

"What the hell do you think you're going to do?" Ralph demanded.

"Going after them. Got to get Miss Callahan."

"You're crazy, Slocum. You can't take on five guns by yourself."

"I kind of figured you two would help."

"That's the sheriff's business."

"You think she'll live long enough for the sheriff to find her?"

"Why would they hurt her?"

"Why'd they take her?"

"But—"

"Look. They killed the driver. They killed her brother. When they're done with her, they'll kill her, too. We're lucky they didn't kill us all."

"It was that one with the shotgun. Pete, they called him. He said there was enough killing. Seemed like he didn't have no stomach for it."

"That'll buy some time, maybe, but that's all." Slocum moved toward the rear of the stage where his horse was tethered. Will Callahan's horse was there, too. They'd taken Maggie's, probably for her to ride.

Slocum untied the chestnut and swung into the saddle. His vision was still a little blurry, and he felt a slight dizziness. Shaking his head to clear it, he asked, "Which way did they go?"

"Slocum, don't do it. You want to do something, go get the sheriff. They see you coming they might kill her just so she don't slow them down."

"They won't see me coming, Winslow. You go get the sheriff. Tell what happened. Tell him I went after them. Tell him whatever the hell you want. I'm through talking." He looked at the shotgun rider. "What's your name?"

The kid poked himself in the chest with a thumb. "Me? Cartwright. Tim Cartwright."

"Cartwright, looks to me like Mr. Winslow's gonna need a little moral support. You best get Mr. Callahan's body into the stage. Can you handle the team?"

"Yes, sir, I can."

"All right then." Slocum wheeled the chestnut, then dug in his spurs. He could see a cloud of dust out across the flats. Two or three miles, he made it, maybe even a little more. Doak wasn't pushing things. He probably figured nobody would bother to follow him.

As long as Doak felt that way, it was best to let him keep on thinking it. But Slocum couldn't close the gap without kicking up a little dust of his own. He only had one canteen. He hefted it, gave it a shake, then let it fall. It was just a little more than half full.

Not knowing the country, he had to keep Doak and his band in sight. For the time being, the dust cloud would do. But once they got into the foothills of the Copper Mountains, he'd lose that advantage. He pushed his horse a little, glancing back over his shoulder. The chestnut was kicking up a little dust, but it thinned quickly and sifted back to the ground rapidly.

Slocum knew the robbers wouldn't bother Maggie until they stopped for the night. Even though they were in no apparent hurry, they wouldn't waste time to attack her until they could be assured of enough leisure.

The Copper Mountains were a smear of darker color rising up out of the arid basin floor. The band of color looked almost perfect, as if it had been drawn by an architect. There was a little more than an hour left before sundown. Slocum wanted to be no more than a mile behind by the time the sun started to slip below the horizon. During twilight, Doak and his men could keep on moving if they wanted to, but Slocum wouldn't be able to see them unless he were very close.

Once they stopped for the night, if they built a fire, it would help, but there was no guarantee they would. In fact, there was no reason to assume they would bother to stop at all. If they knew the terrain, and Slocum was certain they did, they could keep on moving all night long if they chose to.

Keeping one eye on the cloud of dust and one on the sun, Slocum pushed as hard as he could. He was getting closer, but there was a risk that he would be spotted. It was a risk he'd have to take. With little more than fifteen minutes before sundown, the sky was starting to turn an ugly purplish-gray. The few clouds were already darker purple. The sun behind them set their edges on fire for a couple of minutes, until the sun sank even lower; then they turned a purple so dark it was almost black.

The terrain was still spiked with saguaro, but Slocum was aware of the ground starting to slope gently upward. The first of the foothills were less than a mile away. The cactus would begin to give way to juniper and then piñon. The dust cloud was gone. Slocum yanked the canteen off his saddle horn and unscrewed the cap for a drink. He was soaked with sweat, his head ached, and his shoulder still felt as if it were being hammered by an invisible fist.

The water was warm, but it refreshed him a bit as he rinsed the dust away, spat into the dirt, and took a long pull on the tepid water. In the last few minutes of daylight, he pushed the horse even harder, leaning over in the saddle to keep an eye on the trail.

He was heading uphill now. Reaching the crest of the hill, he reined in. He had binoculars and raised them to his eyes to sweep the hilly terrain ahead of him. There wasn't much to see. Already, the valleys were pockets of deep shadow. The ridges were coated with silver that darkened to charcoal even as he watched.

He dropped the glasses and reached for the reins when something caught his eye. Snatching the binoculars again, he trained them on a long, low ridge two valleys over. Two horsemen had just reached the ridgeline. They reined in and turned in the saddle to look down the hill behind them. Slocum recognized one of them as the man with the shotgun, Pete.

Pete's mouth moved soundlessly, then he turned and pointed down into the next valley. A third horsemen bobbed into view, one arm dragging behind him. As he spurred his mount another couple of steps, the reason became apparent. He was pulling on another set of reins. Slocum didn't have to guess who would be on the horse. When Maggie Callahan came into view, he was not surprised.

As near as he could tell, she was unharmed. But if the bandits were getting ready to camp for the night, that might not remain true much longer. He didn't know whether to hope they were making camp or to hope they kept on moving.

He kicked the chestnut and angled down the saguaro-studded slope in front of him. The soil was loose under his mount's hooves, and the animal resisted the prodding of the spurs. Slocum backed off and let the chestnut pick its way downhill.

The shadows were deepening now, and he looked up at the sky once more. The last shafts of sunlight were fading. It would be dark in five minutes. Now came the tricky part. In the darkness, they would be able to hear him when he got close. But if he dismounted and went ahead on foot, he would lose time if they were not camping, and he'd have to wait for morning to pick up the trail.

On the valley floor, he let the chestnut start up the next slope. The horse seemed reluctant to move too quickly, and Slocum found himself getting anxious. He reined in, knowing he was taking a risk, but not knowing what else to do.

Slipping from the saddle, he grabbed the reins and tugged the big chestnut to a nearby saguaro. The giant cactus was so tall its top disappeared in the blackness overhead. Later, when the stars were out, he'd be able to see the top again, but for the moment, there was just too little light.

Looping the reins around the saguaro, he moved along the chestnut's flank and grabbed his Winchester carbine from the saddle boot. There was a box of shells in the saddlbags, and he undid the leather thongs, rooted in the bag until he found the shell box, then flipped it open with a thumb and grabbed a fistful of shells.

Tucking the ammunition into his pocket, he started up the slope. When he reached the top, he stopped to listen. The young night was quiet. If they had stopped, they weren't in the valley below him. He sprinted downhill, keeping one forearm extended to protect himself in case he stumbled. On the valley floor, he stopped again to listen. Still there was silence.

Starting up the next slope, he moved more slowly. If they were in the next shallow valley, silence was essential. Placing each foot carefully, trying to avoid the crunch of the soft stone underfoot, he worked his way uphill. He was still a hundred yards from the ridgeline when he heard the muffled nicker of a horse somewhere ahead.

He dropped into a crouch and moved a little faster. He heard the horse again. He could smell something burning now. Looking up toward the top of the hill, he strained his eyes, but there was still no hint of firelight. But something was definitely burning.

Moving with painstaking care, he covered the last fifty feet one step at a time. He stopped to listen after every step. There was a distant mutter, but so low he couldn't tell whether it was more horses or, possibly, human conversation.

He lay flat and squirmed the last twenty feet, hoping he didn't run across a tarantula, which wouldn't be that dangerous but which would scare the hell out of him, or a sidewinder, which would be dangerous, and would also scare the hell out of him. The sky above him started to brighten. The smell of smoke was stronger, but there was no trace of it visible over the ridge.

Near the top of the ridge, he stopped again to listen. He could hear voices now. They seemed to be arguing, but the words were too indistinct to be certain. Hauling himself the last couple of feet to the top of the hill, he angled toward the left, toward the gnarled trunk of a Joshua. He braced his left shoulder against the tree and raised his head to look down into the valley.

A small fire was still picking up steam. There wasn't much to feed it, and the small branches and twigs were bone dry and burning almost as fast as the men could heap them on. On the far side of the small blaze, he saw Doak. He was talking, arguing probably, with a man whose back was to Slocum. Their voices were strained, but they were obviously trying to keep them down.

Behind Doak, Slocum could just make out the prostrate form of Maggie Callahan. He wasn't too late.

At least, not yet.

4

Slocum felt helpless lying there on the ridge. He counted the flitting shadows; there were five men down there. And they had a trump card in Maggie Callahan. He could pick one or two off with no trouble. But once he opened fire, Maggie would be in danger. Even if they didn't kill her, they would threaten to do so unless he surrendered. If he did, all bets were off. If he didn't, Maggie was as good as dead.

There had to be another way.

He could wait until they were all asleep, but he knew Doak wouldn't leave Maggie alone long enough. He tried to find some other reason for Doak to have brought her along, but he knew before he started that there was none. There was no one to pay a ransom, and that didn't seem to be Doak's style, in any case. She was there for one reason, and one reason alone.

There wasn't a hell of a lot of cover between the ridgeline and the campfire. Getting close would be risky, if not downright impossible. Somehow, he had to get their attention without exposing himself to their weapons.

But how?

Slocum racked his brain, but nothing seemed workable.

There was only one plan that had even a prayer. Backing down the hill, he reached his mount, tugged the horse farther down the hill and angled to the right, where he could conceal the animal a little in a clump of Joshuas. It didn't offer much cover, but it was all he had.

Scouring the barren floor of the valley, he gathered as much firewood as he could find, which wasn't much. Ripping some dead limbs from a dying Joshua, he built a small mound of tinder and kindling, then stacked the few branches, none thicker than his thumb, in three crisscross layers.

Cupping a match in the palms of his hands, he thumbed the head, got it to light, and started the tinder. The pale glow, so faint it was almost swallowed by the night, took its sweet time spreading through the dry moss, finally ignited the dry leaves of the Joshua, then started to flicker as the flames curled around the thick bark.

When he was sure it was going to stay lit, Slocum took four shells for the Winchester and dropped them in among the kindling. Getting to his feet, he sprinted for the ridge, then worked his way parallel about fifteen yards below it, until he was a quarter mile to the right of the campfire in the next shallow valley.

Edging toward the top, he crept over and started to work his way down. He could see the shadowy figures of Doak and his men as they moved around the fire. Slocum knew he would have just a few seconds to make his move once the first shell exploded. He wanted to be on the far side, opposite the sound of the detonating shells, ready to charge in while Doak and his men were distracted. It might even work, Slocum thought.

He reached the floor of the valley, then started up the far side, moving at an angle to bring him behind and above the fire. He had to move cautiously now. The shells could go off at any time, if they went off at all. If they went off before he was in position to capitalize on the slim edge, he would have no choice but to charge ahead and hope for the best.

As he got closer, he could hear angry voices. He couldn't see who was arguing, but there was no mistaking the disagreement. A second later, he heard a shriek, Maggie's voice, and an angry curse. This time he could hear the words: "Bitch tried to claw my eyes out."

Slocum heard the dull impact of a hand on flesh, a punch rather than a slap, and then a second shriek.

"Doak, leave her alone," someone said.

"Mind your own damn business, Pete."

He saw two men now locked together, and heard the grunts as they jockeyed for position. One man broke free and swung his fist.

The first shell went off.

"The hell was that?" somebody shouted. The struggling men stopped circling. One of them, it sounded like Doak, said, "Get on up on that damn hill, Rudy. Take a look."

Another shell went off. There were two left. Slocum heard footsteps pound up the slope. He could see Maggie now, and behind her, an arm circled around her throat, Doak, with his pistol drawn.

Slocum started down the hill, closed the gap enough, and dropped to one knee. The third shell exploded, and Doak shoved Maggie to the ground and sprinted past the fire. Maggie got to her feet slowly, backing away from the flames. All five men were on the far side of it now.

Slocum heard the nicker of horses, the restless thudding of nervous hooves. The animals were beyond the firelight, and he couldn't see them. Maggie kept backing up the hill and Slocum angled across the slope, trying to get in behind her. She tripped and fell, then scrambled back to her feet as Slocum reached a point directly behind her.

He didn't want to shout. Hissing a loud whisper, he called to her. "Maggie. Up here!" She stopped in her tracks, confused. She turned to peer uphill into the blackness.

"Where you going, bitch?" Doak shouted. Slocum heard footsteps, then saw two men racing toward the fire. He dropped to one knee again, and raised the Winchester. Picking the nearer of the two, he squeezed the trigger.

The sharp crack of the Winchester seemed to freeze everything except the man in its sights. He stumbled and skidded on his stomach toward the fire. Doak shouted, then started to raise his pistol.

Slocum fired again. He saw a puff of dust as his bullet went wide. Doak stopped in his tracks, then started to backpedal. Maggie scrambled up the slope toward Slocum, holding the tatters of her dress over her chest. She saw Slocum and clutched at his arm, but he swept her behind him and jacked another shell into the Winchester's chamber.

Without looking at her, he hissed, "Keep going. Get over the hill. And don't stop, no matter what happens. I'll find you."

The last shell went off, and he knew he was out of time. It wouldn't take long for the bandits to realize there was no one on the far side of the hill. Slocum started to back up the hill, stopping twice to fire the Winchester, but Doak had scrambled out of range into the darkness.

He knew the outlaws couldn't see him now, and he turned and sprinted for the top of the hill. Taking cover just over the ridge, he called to Maggie in a low voice. "You all right?" he asked.

There was no answer. He tried again. This time, he heard a whimper, somewhere below him in the darkness. "Maggie," he hissed. "Are you all right?"

Between sobs, she managed to say, "I guess so."

He wanted to go to her, but he had to watch the slope. Before making his next move, he wanted to know what Doak was planning. The man he'd shot lay facedown, just inside the circle of firelight, but he couldn't see any of the others.

He heard shouts, but the words were garbled. All they told him was a rough idea of the location of the four men he couldn't see.

He reloaded the Winchester, staring down into the darkness. He tried to listen for some indication of what they were planning, but the shouts had died away. For several minutes, he heard nothing. Then a horse nickered. It was off to his right. Slocum heard a noise on the slope behind him and cast a quick glance over his shoulder. Maggie was crawling toward him. Her shadow was just discernible in the dark.

"Are you okay?" he whispered. "Did they hurt you?"

"No." The husky voice trembled, but she was no longer on the edge of hysteria. "Will is dead, isn't he?"

"Yes." So short a word, and yet it meant so much. "Yes, he's dead."

He heard one sob, then nothing. She crept closer then, and he felt her hand on his leg. He slid downhill a couple of feet. "I have a horse, but we can't leave yet. We'll never outrun them if we try. Better to wait here, see what they'll do."

"You should kill them, all of them, for what they did to Will." Her voice was so cold, so hard, now. It didn't seem possible it could be the same woman he'd spoken to on the stage.

"I know how you feel, but the only thing we should be concerned with is getting you home safe."

"I know. But I hate it. I hate that I'm so helpless. I hate that there's nothing we can do. I hate that Will is dead."

He was about to answer her when he heard a whinny and the pounding of hooves. He scrambled back toward the ridge. He saw one horse race past the campfire, its hooves scattering sand and gravel down the slope until it disappeared. A moment later, he heard another horse, then a third.

"What are they doing?" Maggie asked.

"I don't know. They've mounted up, but I can't see them. I don't know if they're going to charge us or if they're going to make a run for it."

"I hope they charge us. Do you have a gun I can use?"

"Maggie, if they do charge us, it's all over. But I don't think they will. I don't think they'll take the chance. Not in the dark. But if they wait till morning, they'll have us. We have to get out of here."

It grew quiet. Slocum strained to hear in the darkness, but he knew, long before he'd permit himself to believe it, that the bandits had gone. The hoofbeats had long since died away. If they had ridden off and dismounted to come back and mount a search on foot, the outlaws might stumble on them by accident.

"We should move out of here," Slocum whispered. "They might be coming back. Where were the horses?"

She crept back up to lie beside him. He was aware of her warmth in the chilly night air. "There." She pointed to the right of the fire. "That's where they were."

"You wait here. I'm going to go down and see if they left your mount."

"Don't, please. Don't leave me here alone."

Slocum hesitated. Even though he understood her terror, he didn't want to expose her to the risk. But she snatched the decision away from him. "I'm coming with you," she said. "Let's go."

Knowing he would gain nothing by arguing, Slocum agreed. "All right, but you stay close and don't talk."

He stood up and shifted the Winchester to his left hand. Reaching down to help Maggie up, he felt again the strength of that soft hand. As she straightened, she lost her balance for a second, and the tatters of the bodice fell away. Even in the darkness, he could sense her embarrassment, and was aware, too, of the shadowy contours. She snatched the scraps of cloth together and held them across her chest.

Neither of them spoke. He turned and started downhill, placing his feet carefully, listening to the night, hoping he would hear nothing. As they drew close, he heard the thud of a hoof on the arid ground. The horse sensed their presence. Slocum sighed with relief. At least they wouldn't have to double up.

When they got closer, a second horse loomed out of the dark. He had forgotten the man he'd shot. The second horse must have been his mount. He helped Maggie into the saddle and took the second horse by the reins.

Walking back toward the fire, he halted just on the edge

of the circle of light. "Wait here," he whispered. He walked toward the prostrate body. As he got near, he saw the back rising and falling. The man was still alive. There was an ugly stain on the back of his shirt, just below the armpit. Slocum knelt and turned the man over.

He could see that the wound, while bleeding heavily, was not fatal. Without thinking, he tore the man's shirt into pieces and bound the wound. When he straightened up, his hands were full of blood. He bent to scoop up some dirt and rubbed it over the blood, then rubbed harder to scrape away the bloody soil.

When he turned back to Maggie, she was on the ground. The ruined dress was down around her ankles. He watched as she stepped out of it, tugged her knickers down and stepped free. She must have sensed his eyes on her. She backed away a bit farther from the dying fire. Moving more quickly, she slipped into a checkered shirt. Then, taking a pair of jeans from her saddlebag, she bent to step into them. The shirt hung open, and her breasts swayed with the vigorous motion.

She pulled the jeans up, buttoned them, and pulled the shirt close. Only then did she look at him.

He didn't know the meaning of her faint smile.

5

Slocum hoisted the bound and bandaged outlaw onto the horse. He took the reins and walked uphill, Maggie Callahan riding her own mount right behind him. When he reached the ridge, he looked back at the dying fire, then moved on over the ridge and started down. The sky was brightening as the moon started to rise. He thanked his stars it would soon be possible to see a hand in front of his face.

Angling across the downward slope, he kept leaning forward, trying to pick out the clump of trees where his chestnut had been tethered. He could hear his horse before he could see it. Coiling the reins of the bandit's horse in his hand, he stopped and waited for Maggie to come abreast of him. When she was close enough, he handed her the reins.

"Wait here," he said.

"Where are you going?" She was trying to keep the fear out of her voice, but not succeeding.

"Just want to get my horse. I'll be right back."

"All right, but please hurry."

He didn't answer. Rather than credit her fear, he wanted to ignore it, hoping she would do the same. He could move faster without the horse in tow, and it took him under five minutes to locate the chestnut. Booting the Winchester with more violence than was necessary, he swung into the saddle and nudged the big stallion back uphill.

The moon came up abruptly. Rising over the flat wasteland behind him, it spilled its silver light over his back and shoulders, casting a dull shadow of horse and rider on the sandy ground ahead of him.

Maggie saw him coming and called out. "Slocum?"

"Who else would it be?" he asked.

"That's not funny."

"It wasn't meant to be, Maggie. There's no point in getting yourself all worked up. They're gone."

"Yes, they're gone. But my brother is still dead, so it hasn't changed things very much, has it?"

"You know I didn't mean to suggest that. But we have a difficult ride ahead of us. If he wakes up," and here he jutted his chin toward the trussed and still unconscious outlaw, "we'll have our hands full. I have to know whether or not I can count on you."

"Oh, you can count on me, Mr. Slocum. Those bastards are going to pay for what they did to Will. Even if I have to find them myself, they'll pay."

"I wouldn't count on anybody but him paying, Miss Callahan. I don't think the rest of them will bother to help him out."

"But you don't know that, do you?"

"No, I don't know that."

"Well, then—?"

"We better get moving." He nudged his mount closer to Maggie, then reached out for the reins of the outlaw's horse. "I'll take care of him," he said.

"I wish you would. But you won't."

He knew what she meant. He understood her hatred, but he couldn't afford to let it take control of her. "You don't really mean that. And even if you do, you should understand that the law has its place. Ignore that, and you make more men like him possible."

"What I had in mind was making one fewer man like him."

"I know."

"You really wouldn't do that, would you? I can see that. Tell me, Mr. Slocum, is it because you don't have the courage for it, or is it really against your conscience?"

Slocum didn't dignify the question with so much as a grunt. It didn't take courgae to shoot a defenseless man, and if Maggie Callahan didn't already know that, telling her so wouldn't make a whole lot of difference. He snatched the reins from her hand and nudged the chestnut into a walk.

The moon was a mixed blessing. Slocum looked up at it, noticed it was nearly full, and realized it would help him to be seen as much as it would help him see. He didn't think Doak and his men were likely to be hunting for him and Maggie, but he didn't want to get overconfident.

Out in the open, there was not much they could do to cover themselves, but it wasn't light enough, and it was too far, to push the horses flat out and hope to get all the way back to Yuma at a gallop. And having the wounded man in tow slowed them even more. Part of Slocum wanted to leave the man behind. The decision to bring him along wasn't made out of any misplaced humanitarianism. The man was a robber, he had participated in two cold-blooded murders, and he could name his accomplices. That made him the most important witness to the afternoon's events.

But that would also occur to Doak. He must have felt reasonably confident that the man was dead, or he wouldn't have left him behind. Or would he?

They had been riding for half an hour when Maggie pushed her horse up alongside Slocum's chestnut. She rode in silence for several minutes. Slocum watched her from the corner of his eye. It seemed like she wanted to tell him something, but either wasn't ready or didn't know how. Rather than push the point, he decided to ride it out. Maggie would find the words or she wouldn't.

After ten minutes, Slocum reined in, catching Maggie by surprise.

"Why are we stopping?"

"We have got to give the horses a break. They've been ridden pretty hard today. We run into Doak, they'll need a little extra."

"You don't think we will, though, do you?"

He sensed the uncertainty in the question, as if Maggie didn't know whether she ought to be glad or disappointed. "No, I don't."

"Then why are we stopping?"

"What I think and what will happen might not be the same thing, Miss Callahan."

"Maggie."

"I'd prefer to stick with Miss Callahan, if you don't mind. I'm not all that comfortable calling someone I hardly know by her first name."

"Anyone, or just me?"

He knew that when he thought of her, it was Maggie, but when he spoke to her, it was stiffly formal. The distinction probably meant something, but for the time being it was something he didn't want to discuss. "Anyone," he told her.

"Whatever you say, Mr. Slocum." She fell quiet, then slipped from the saddle. He watched her strecth her long legs, dropping slowly into a squat, then straightening again. "I'm not very used to riding," she said, when she noticed him watching her.

"Can you manage?"

"Do I have a choice?"

"No."

"Then I'll manage."

In the pale moonlight he couldn't be sure, but he thought she smiled. He opened his canteen and took a mouthful, spat, then swallowed a second mouthful. He nodded and she stepped closer to take the offered canteen. "I can't get used to this climate," she said.

"You got to be an Apache or a fool to get used to it, I think."

"Are you used to it?" She took a swig and handed the canteen back to him.

He laughed. "I guess you got me there, Miss Callahan. Yes, I suppose I'm used to it."

She grew suddenly quiet. He slid out of the saddle. She turned away, walked a few steps, then stopped. She hugged her arms to her chest. He took a step toward her, but she shook her head.

Slocum felt suddenly helpless. It was not a feeling he was used to. And not one he liked. He wanted to say something, but there was nothing he could say that would mean anything.

She turned back to him, but stayed where she was. When she spoke, her voice was just above a whisper. "I can't believe I'll never see Will again. I just can't believe it. Why did they have to shoot him?"

Slocum knew there was no answer to that question. Maggie knew it, too, but they both knew it was a question that had to be asked.

"I remember once when we were children. He fell down and hurt himself. Cut his chin very badly. I don't suppose you noticed it, no reason you should have, really, but there was a small scar on his jaw, right on the bone. At least it seems small now, but when it happened, I thought it was the end of the world. There was blood all over. He was my big brother and I thought he was going to die. I was terrified. It's strange. Now he's dead, and I can't believe it."

She walked past him and stood with her arms folded, staring at the back of the unconscious outlaw. She raised one hand clenched in a fist, and he thought she was about to strike the wounded man. Instead, she pounded the fist on her thigh again and again.

Slocum grabbed her arm. "Miss Callahan, stop it. You've got to get control of yourself."

She wrenched the hand free, then struck him in the chest once, then again even harder. "No, no, no I don't! I don't want to control myself. It's not fair."

She took a step back and he reached for her, afraid she was going to run off. As his fingers closed over her wrist, he felt all the tension drain out of her, then she curled toward him, her back against his chest, and hugged his arm in both of hers.

"I'm sorry," she whispered. "I'm sorry."

"You have nothing to be sorry about, Miss Callahan, just—"

She was shaking then, and it came pouring out of her in a torrent. He felt the tears splashing on his wrists and the backs of his hands. He held her, not too close, but close enough to let her know she was safe. It seemed to last forever, but it was over so suddenly, a moment later it was as if it had never happened.

She turned and looked up at him. "I suppose we'd better go," she said.

Slocum nodded.

She moved back to her horse and swung into the saddle with the grace of a born rider. She flashed him a weak smile, all but washed out by the indifferent light of the moon.

When he was back in the saddle, she said, "Did you ever lose someone you loved? Someone who meant more to you than life itself?"

"Yes." It was that simple. He had never had the question put so bluntly. And had never allowed himself so direct an answer. But it was true. "Yes," he said again.

She nodded. "It gets better someday, doesn't it?"

Slocum didn't answer.

"Please tell me it does."

Slocum rubbed at his chin. The scrape of rough skin on whiskers was the only sound.

He reached down to snag the reins of the outlaw's horse. He noticed the gunman, still unconscious, his breathing still shallow, rasping in his throat. He wondered how Maggie had resisted the urge to flail at the bandit with both fists. He wondered if he would have had such self-control. There was steel in Maggie Callahan, and all he could do was shake his head in wonder.

"You ready?" he asked.

She nodded that she was, and he prodded the chestnut, still shaking his head.

6

The ride back to Yuma took them past the notch where
the stage had been hit. In the moonlight, Slocum could
see bloodstains on the ground. He tried to maneuver his
mount between the ugly reminder and Maggie Callahan,
but it didn't work. She had seen it. Slocum looked at her,
but didn't say anything. Her face became a grim mask for
a moment, and she glanced at the wounded man, now conscious and moaning. The mask slipped for a split second,
and Slocum wondered when he had ever seen such hate
in so beautiful a countenance. And he knew the answer.
Never.

The moon started to slip, but the sky was already turning
gray as sunup approached. Slocum stopped once more to
rèst the animals. This time, Maggie stayed on her horse.
She refused the canteen when he offered it with a shake of
her head.

The outlaw twisted his head to look at Slocum. "Thirsty,"
he croaked.

Slocum looked at him, shrugged, and stepped to the prisoner. The man turned his head to one side, and Slocum let
a bit of water trickle out of the canteen. The man swallowed

greedily, smacked his lips, and waited for a second swallow. Slocum obliged him.

"What's your name?" he asked, when the prisoner was done drinking.

"Bradley, Tom Bradley." Slocum studied the ravaged face. The man was barely twenty. He lacked the hard edges Doak had shown, but there was something in the eyes, some emptiness, as if something was missing inside him.

"Well, Mr. Bradley," Slocum said, "you have bought yourself a mess of trouble."

"What're you gonna do with me?" Bradley asked.

"Not up to me. That's for the judge to decide."

Bradley nodded. Hanging upside down from the saddle, it was an odd gesture. Slocum shook his head. He screwed the lid back on the canteen and made a move to walk back to his horse.

"I didn't shoot nobody. You were there. You seen it. I didn't shoot nobody."

"Yeah, I saw it. And if it was up to me, Mr. Bradley, you'd be pulling a good rope a little out of shape right now. But it's not up to me, like I said. So we'll just have to see whether the judge gives a good goddamn whether you pulled the trigger or not."

"Wasn't supposed to be no shooting."

"You expected the driver would just hand over the money, just like that?"

"Doak said—"

"The hell with Doak," Maggie screamed. "The hell with you, too. If I had a gun, I'd—"

"Let it be, Miss Callahan," Slocum said. "We're almost there. We'll turn him over to the sheriff and you can get some rest."

"I don't want rest, Slocum. I want my brother back. But I can't have that, so I'll settle for the next best thing."

Slocum walked to her horse and stood looking up at her. "Miss Callahan, it's been a long day. You've been through a lot. Maybe you—"

"Don't patronize me, Mr. Slocum."

She was right, and he knew it. Patting her horse on the neck, he turned and walked back to his own mount. Swinging up into the saddle, he looked at the prisoner once more. That emptiness in Bradley's eyes bothered him more than he was willing to admit.

Spurring the chestnut, he led the way as the moon finally disappeared and the sky grew bright. For the next hour, no one spoke. The sun began to seep over the horizon like red water spilling over the top of a well. They were on the road now, close to Yuma. He was dead tired, and all he could think about was getting some sleep.

Watching Maggie, he realized that sleep was the farthest thing from her mind. She was running on some bottomless source of energy. Her eyes were bright, and her hands played nervously with the reins. He knew that the anxiety of the afternoon and the rage that so far had had no release were screwing her nerves tighter and tighter. If something didn't happen soon to release that tension, she would snap. He hoped to God that it didn't happen before they reached town.

The sun was well up in the sky by the time Yuma appeared on the horizon. At first, it was a shimmering mirage under the early sun, already hammering down on Slocum's back. As it materialized, it seemed not quite real, with no more substance than a house of cards. It was the last town of any significance before Mexico to the south and California to the west. Yuma seemed tenuous, fragile almost, as if the first stiff breeze would reduce it to a collection of brittle sticks and bone-dry chips of wood.

At the outskirts of the town, Slocum stopped one final time. He tried to get Maggie's attention, but she was in another world. Her bright green eyes danced, never stood still long enough to fasten on any one thing. Slocum wasn't sure whether she was deliberately ignoring him or just so completely absorbed in her own thoughts that she failed to notice him. She rode right past him, and he had to reach out and snatch at her reins before she paid any attention to him.

"Miss Callahan, I'll find the sheriff. I think you should go on and take a room at the hotel. Do you have enough money?"

"Don't worry about me, Mr. Slocum. I can take care of myself. It seems I'll have to from now on, after all." She tossed one last bitter look at Bradley, then nudged her horse back into a walk. Slocum watched her for a minute, then urged his own mount forward.

The town was nearly deserted. A few horses were tied up along the dusty main street, but there wasn't a soul in sight. There was no noise except the steady clop of Maggie Callahan's horse, growing fainter as she pulled away.

In front of the sheriff's office, he dismounted. Leaving Bradley draped over the saddle, he climbed onto the boardwalk. The shade of the *ramada* gave him some relief from the already oppressive sun. The door of the sheriff's office was open, and Slocum stepped inside.

A man was asleep at the desk, head resting on folded arms. He wore no hat, and a small bald spot gleamed in a shaft of sunlight stabbing through the dusty window. Slocum cleared his throat and, when that failed to wake the man, reached back to rap on the doorframe.

The man sprang up like a jack-in-the-box, trying to look alert, but the confused look on his red and wrinkled face was proof to the contrary. A star glittered on his chest, its bright flashes replacing the steady gleam of the bald spot.

"You the sheriff?" Slocum asked.

The man shook his head. "Name's Brady Anderson. Deputy. Sheriff Macomb's to home." He looked at a clock on the wall, then back to Slocum. "Most likely still sleeping, I expect, judging by the hour. He was up half the night. Can I help you with something, Mr.—?"

"Slocum. I guess you already know about the robbery?"

"The stage? Hell, yes. Two men killed, too. What about it?" He ran a fistful of stubby fingers across his cheeks, trying to press out the lines engraved into the slack flesh by the folds of his shirtsleeves. He pursed his mouth as if to rid it of an unpleasant taste.

"I got one of the robbers outside."

"You what?"

"I got one of the robbers outside."

"How you know that? Who is he?"

"Says his name's Tom Bradley. And I know he's one of them because I was on the stage."

"What'd you say your name was?"

"John Slocum."

"No wonder that sounded familiar. You're the guy went after that little gal they run off with, ain't you? You got her, too? She all right?"

Slocum nodded. "She's all right—under the circumstances."

"They—didn't do nothing to her—did they?"

Slocum shook his head. "No."

"Where's she at? Gonna need a statement from her."

"She went on down to the hotel. She's been through a lot."

"Course she has. But we got to get a statement, while it's still fresh in her mind. I got to get the sheriff." He got up from behind the desk. He seemed more alert now, whether because he was shaking off the grogginess of sleep or because he had been galvanized by the news, Slocum couldn't tell.

"It can wait till this afternoon, I would think."

"You think so? I better let the sheriff decide. I mean, I don't want to bother her or nothing. But—"

"Why don't we get Bradley in here. Then you can decide what to do about the rest of it. He's hurt some."

"Shot the bastard, did you? I knew Jake Dalton, you know. Sumbitches shouldn't have gone and shot that old man. Nicest man you could want to meet. Never hurt nobody in his life. Let's go take a look at this bastard."

He stepped around the desk, snatching his hat from a wooden rack on the wall and clapping it on his head in a single, practiced motion. He led Slocum outside. Stepping into the street, he walked around the back of the horse, resting one hand on its rump and clapping the animal absently.

Bradley turned his head to look up at the deputy.

"I seen him around some," Anderson said. "Never knew his name, though." He dropped to one knee. Seeing the rope securing Bradley's hands to his feet, Anderson reached into his pocket and withdrew a clasp knife. When he pulled it open, the blade locked with an audible click. Without paying any particular attention, he reached under the horse's midsection and severed the rope.

Anderson stood up, closed the knife by pressing the back of the blade on Bradley's spine, then pocketed it again. Without ceremony, he grabbed Bradley by the belt and tugged him off the horse, letting him land in a heap on the street. Bradley struggled to get up, and Anderson reached down to haul him to his feet.

"You certain this is one of 'em, Slocum?"

"Yeah, I'm certain."

"You the one shot him?"

Slocum nodded.

"Shoulda killed him. I woulda. What he done to old Jake. He pull a trigger?"

"No."

"Don't matter. That gal, her brother was the other one got killed, wasn't he?"

"Yes, he was."

"Reason I ask, her friend, Ralph somebody, took care of the body. Took Callahan to Parsons's, that's the mortician. He's staying at the hotel, too. Ralph, that is. Not the mortician. That's Daniel Parsons. He lives outside of town, over toward Pinon."

He shoved Bradley then. "Watch your step, cowboy," he said, pushing the prisoner again, then waiting for Bradley to climb up onto the boardwalk.

Anderson kept prodding Bradley with stiff fingers until he entered the office, then passed on into the cellblock beyond. Slocum stood in the doorway and watched the door swing closed. Anderson moved back to the front office. "I guess he'll need a doc to look at that wound. I'll stop there after I get Sheriff Macomb. Take me awhile. You can wait here, if you want."

"Thanks, I will," Slocum said. He sat down behind the desk. Through the window, he watched Anderson mount and ride off.

7

Slocum was getting angrier by the minute as he waited for the sheriff to arrive. It was almost an hour before a big man in faded denims, a star pinned to his pocket, strode in the front door. Behind him were Brady Anderson, Ralph Winslow, and Tim Cartwright, the shotgun rider from the stage. The man's deeply creased and sun-darkened skin looked as if it wouldn't permit a smile. In any case, he was all business.

"You Slocum?" he asked as he took off his hat and clapped it on a peg on the hat rack.

Slocum nodded, stood up from behind the desk, and made room for him. The sheriff stuck out a huge hand. "Vance Macomb," he said. "Now, suppose we get down to cases."

"Fine by me."

"How come you was on the stage? Why not just ride that fine animal you got outside?"

"Sheriff, you spend as much time in the saddle as I do, a chance to go someplace any other way is more than welcome."

"Fair enough. Now, you mind telling me what happened out there yesterday?"

"Not at all. Five men stopped the stage. They killed the driver and one passenger. They took a couple of bags from a strongbox. I don't know what was in them, but they seemed to know the bags would be on the stage, and I assume they did know what was in them. They said as much. Near as I can tell, that was the reason they were there. The killings were not part of the plan."

The sheriff lowered his massive frame into the desk chair. Slocum expected it to squeak in protest, but the only noise was the scrape of cartridges on the chair's leather back. Macomb looked at him for a moment, his head tilted to one side a bit. "You ever see any of these men before?"

"Nope."

"You sure?"

"I'm sure."

"How come they didn't shoot you?"

"How would I know the answer to that?"

"You mean to say you were just lucky? That it?"

"What are you getting at, Sheriff?"

"Not getting at anything, Mr. Slocum. I just want to know exactly what happened. I got to figure out why, and the more I know, the easier that is. Now, what happened next? I already heard it from Ralph, here, and from Cartwright, but I want to hear it from you."

"They were bothering the woman passenger, and—"

"That would be Miss Callahan, the sister of one of the victims, that right?"

"That's right, yes. Anyhow, I tried to stop them, and I got coldcocked. When I came to, they were gone, and so was Miss Callahan. I tracked them, and got her back."

"And in the process, you winged one of the bastards and brought him in along with the woman, that right?"

"That's right, yes."

Macomb leaned back in the chair until its back touched the wall behind him. He rubbed his chin with a handful of stiff, thick fingers. There was no beard visible, so the hissing sound must have been callused fingers on leathery chin.

"Tell me something, Mr. Slocum. How come you didn't see fit to wait for help before you lit out after them? You could have got yourself killed, and the woman, too. You understand that, don't you?"

"Yeah, I understand that. But it was pretty clear what they had in mind, one of them, anyhow, a man they called Doak. It was also pretty clear that Doak didn't give a damn what happened to the woman after that. I figured they might kill her or leave her in the desert, which would amount to the same thing."

"So you played one-man cavalry and rode to the rescue, that it?"

"I wouldn't put it that way, no."

"Then how *would* you put it?"

"Look, Sheriff, I don't think I care for the tone of your questions. The woman was in danger. I was there; I did what I thought was right. If that's a crime, then lock me up; if it isn't, then I could use some sleep."

"Now don't be gettin' all testy, Mr. Slocum. I just—"

"Sheriff, I really don't give a damn. If you'll excuse me, now I have to find a room."

"Slocum, don't high-hat me. Understand, I'm not saying I don't admire what you done. Because if you done what it looks like, you got more guts than most. And I got to wonder why you didn't have more help goin' after Miss Callahan." He looked pointedly at Winslow and Cartwright before continuing. But there's something about all this don't sit right, and I intend to find out why. If you know anything, now's the time to tell me. You won't get a second chance."

"Good morning, Sheriff. I'll be at the hotel, if you want to talk to me again."

"I will, Mr. Slocum. I most certainly will. And I'm going to have to ask that you not leave town until this mess is cleared up. Circuit judge'll be here next week. We should be able to take care of it then."

Slocum touched the brim of his hat with a couple of fingers and stepped out into the bright sunshine. He swung into the saddle and glanced back at the open door of the sheriff's office. He could see Macomb watching him, still seated in his chair.

Nudging the chestnut into a walk, he moved down the street toward Yuma's two hotels. He wondered about Macomb's hostility and decided there had to be more to the situation than he understood. He wanted to know what was in the two canvas bags, but Macomb hadn't said, and he wasn't about to ask. He'd find out soon enough; that much was certain.

He stopped in front of the first hotel, a place called Royce's Hotel, and dismounted. The chestnut fidgeted. He knew the horse was hungry and thirsty, but he wanted to make sure he had someplace to sleep before he found a livery stable.

The hotel lobby smelled of cut flowers. Two large vases full of roses stood on small tables tucked into opposite corners. Thick sofas, edged in gold brocade, lined one wall. The carpet underfoot was halfway between brand new and threadbare, but it was clean, and that spoke well for the accommodations.

The clerk signed him in, then said, "I have a message for you."

"For me?"

"Yes, sir, a Miss Margaret Callahan said she wanted to see you as soon as you checked in." The clerk, a skinny man who seemed overworked just supporting the thick red walrus mustache that all but obscured his mouth, winked at him. "Good-looking woman, that Miss Callahan. You're one lucky cowboy." His mouth twisted from a dim smile to a leer.

"You know something, mister?"

"What's that, Mr. Slocum?"

"I tell Miss Callahan you said that, and I wouldn't give a plugged nickel you still have that fancy mustache come sundown."

One hand drifted upward to stroke the thick bush. The clerk took a step back as if Slocum had threatened him with bodily harm.

Slocum smiled then. "Course, you might look a whole lot better without it, anyway."

"Hey, I didn't mean nothing. I mean, she—I thought that—"

"You best leave off thinking for a few days, get your head in order."

"Yes, sir, Mr. Slocum. I'm sorry."

Slocum stood there, his fingers drumming on the desk. "Well—" he said.

"Well, what, Mr. Slocum?"

"What room is Miss Callahan in?"

Still flustered, he shook his head. It took a second for the question to sink in. "Oh," he said then, "she's in 206. Down the end of the hall."

Slocum glanced at the key in his fist. It was for 208, probably right next to Maggie Callahan's room. "Thanks," Slocum said. He moved toward the curving stairway and climbed the stairs two at a time. When he reached the second-floor landing, he glanced down at the desk. The clerk was watching him apprehensively. Slocum waved and turned down the hall.

Room 206 was the next to the last room on the right. That meant 208 was a corner room. Probably too light for him to get much sleep, but it was too late to worry about that now. He tapped on the door to 206. When he heard no response, he rapped a little harder.

From inside, he heard a muffled voice. "Just a minute—"

Footsteps approached, and the knob rattled in its channel for a second before the latch clicked. The door swung open and he saw Maggie, one hand combing through tangled red curls. Her face was puffy and, even in the dim light of a single coal-oil lamp, he could see the redness around her eyes. She stepped back to let him in.

"You all right?" Slocum asked.

She nodded, swallowed hard, and closed the door after he entered. "Yes."

She was lying and she knew he knew it. She walked to the window and pulled the curtains aside to let in the sun.

Then, sitting on the edge of the bed, she pointed to a chair over against the wall. As the sun washed over her, it was obvious that she had been crying almost since she'd arrived. She toyed with her upper lip, tracing it with the tip of her tongue.

"You wanted to see me," Slocum prompted.

"Yes. I did." She nodded vigorously. "Thank you for coming."

"Bradley's all locked away. The sheriff says there'll most likely be a trial next week."

"I know. He told me."

"You saw him already?"

She nodded. "Yes. He was here for ten minutes or so. Ralph Winslow was with him, and another man, a deputy, I think."

"How'd you find him?"

"What do you mean?"

"Polite? Rude? Helpful?"

"Distant, I suppose, maybe even a little suspicious. I don't know why. I mean, he didn't accuse me of anything, but it seemed like he wanted to. I don't know—"

"Treated me the same way. I think it has something to do with the robbery, though, not the shootings."

"What was taken?"

"He didn't say, and I didn't ask."

"Ralph wasn't too talkative. I wanted to ask him about Will's—my brother's body, but I didn't get a chance. I—would you help me? I want to see that he's given a decent burial, but I couldn't stand to have that windbag involved."

"Of course," Slocum said. "When?"

"The sooner the better, I guess." She twisted the fingers on one hand in the fingers of the other. It looked almost as if she were trying to unscrew them from their sockets.

Slocum stood up. "I can go now, if you want. Tell the undertaker you'll be by later. If that would help."

"No." The word snapped like a tiny whip in the small room. "I mean, I have to do it. If I wait, it'll just be harder to do. I want to get it behind me."

"Whatever you want, Miss Callahan."

She tried to smile at him, but it failed miserably. "Thank you, Mr. Slocum. I appreciate it."

She stood then, and walked to a small dresser. Sitting down, she reached over to turn up the lamp wick and then took a brush and started to untangle the wild red cascade of her hair. Four or five vicious strokes later, she slammed the brush onto the dresser. "I guess it doesn't matter what I look like, does it?" She watched him in the mirror.

"No, ma'am, it doesn't," he said.

8

The hour at the mortician's was one Slocum hoped to God he never had to repeat. Maggie Callahan swung like a pendulum, alternately weeping and raging. The mortician seemed unfazed by it all, as if it happened every day. Maybe, Slocum thought, in his line of work, it did. But he was welcome to it.

Maggie had gone back to her room, almost at gunpoint. She didn't want to go, but Slocum pointed out there was no place else for her *to* go. It occurred to him that in similar circumstances, a man most likely would go out and get drunk. And if he got really lucky, someone would oblige him with a fistfight. But women didn't have that luxury. If they wanted to get rid of the pain chewing at their guts like angry rats, they had no choice but to rant and rave. Not fair, really, but that's just the way it was.

With Maggie safely lodged in her room, at least for the moment, and his horse finally quartered at the livery stable, maybe he could get some rest. Slocum was hungry, but he thought he just might be too tired to chew anything firmer than apple sauce.

The clerk watched him fearfully as he crossed the lobby and started up the stairs. When he entered the long hallway on the second floor, he thought he could hear a whispered conversation somewhere below him. There hadn't been anyone in the lobby other than the clerk, and it struck him as odd, almost as if someone had been hiding, and resumed talking only after he was out of sight and, presumably, earshot.

He stood there for a few moments, but the conversation, if that's what it was, died away. All he could hear now was the sound of traffic in the street, the creak of a wagon as it passed, and the steady thudding of hooves. He thought about going back to the lobby, but shrugged the impulse off and moved down the hall to his room.

As he passed room 206, he heard Maggie still snuffling, and he wondered whether he ought to knock. But she needed sleep. If he left her alone, maybe she would wear herself out and drift off for a few hours.

He stopped at his own room with one hand on the knob. He thought for a moment he heard something inside. Turning the knob slowly, he heard another soft thud, almost certainly inside. Drawing his Colt Navy, he eased the door open, keeping away from the open doorway. Flat against the wall to the left of the doorway, he tilted his head just enough to see inside. Unlike Maggie's room, his was bright, with windows on both sides.

It looked to be empty, but he wasn't about to take a chance. Ducking across the opening, he tensed, waiting for a gunshot, but nothing happened. He bent at the waist and darted inside. Both windows were open. He tried to remember if they had been open when he left, but he wasn't sure. He'd only been inside long enough to drop his saddlebags. They were still in a heap on the floor near the bed, right where he'd left them.

Stepping to the rear window, he poked his head through the filmy curtains. A narrow wooden porch ran the width of the building, and had a stairway at one end. The porch was as deserted as his room. He heard a horse down below, but his view was blocked by the balcony.

Ducking through the window, he stepped onto the porch

and leaned over the frail-looking railing. He caught a glimpse of a horseman just turning a corner, but the man seemed to be in no hurry. If he had been in Slocum's room, he didn't seem as if he was worried about being spotted.

Crawling back into his room, Slocum realized he was letting the sheriff's attitude and his own vague unease play tricks with his mind. He was jumping at shadows, hearing noises that meant nothing, if they were even there.

Back inside, he closed the door to the hallway, turned the rather insignificant latch, and sat down on the bed. He took off his gun belt, placed it on the floor, then lay back. He thought about taking his boots off, couldn't decide, and finally sat up to do it. He was too tired to be going anywhere for the next few hours, and he might as well make himself as comfortable as possible.

A bath appealed to him, but it could wait. The room was so bright that when he lay back down, he draped a forearm over his eyes to shield them from the glare. The curtains moved in the hot breeze. He could hear the stiff lace scratching against the windowsill.

Letting the sound lull him, he drifted off to sleep. He woke frequently, thinking he'd heard something. Each time, he'd lie there listening, his arm over the side of the bed and his fingers curled around the butt of the Colt. But each time, the sound, if there had been one, was not repeated.

When the sun started to go down, he woke once more, this time knowing that he was not going to be able to go back to sleep. Slocum wasn't refreshed; his sleep had been too fitful, but he knew that his nerves were too skittish to get any more rest.

He lay there on the bed, watching the white heat of the afternoon turn quickly to the dull orange of evening. The color splashed through the windows like water, staining everything it touched. The curtains looked as if they had caught fire.

The breeze was still there, and it was just as hot as it had been. He sat up in bed and stripped off his shirt, then walked to the washstand, poured a pitcher of tepid water into the basin, and scrubbed himself down. He left his pants on, thinking to change them later, after he'd had something to eat.

Taking a clean shirt from his saddlebags, he slipped it on, pressed a few of the wrinkles out with the flat of his hand, and buttoned it up. Walking back to the bed, he retrieved his gun belt, buckled it on, and snatched the room key from the nightstand.

Downstairs, he crossed the lobby toward the open front door. The night clerk was on duty, and paid no attention to him as he stepped out into the last of the day's sunlight. It was still hot, hotter than he remembered, hotter than he hoped. Already, he could feel the thin glaze of sweat on his skin.

There was a small restaurant in town, a block away, and he headed for it, thinking to get something to eat before it closed. When he got there, he saw the Closed sign already in place. That left one of the half-dozen saloons. He could get something to eat there, although not much, but since it was the only choice, he had no difficulty making it.

He looked for a saloon that seemed peaceful. He was not in the mood for a rowdy bunch. The Double Spur looked like it would do, and he pushed through the butterfly doors enough to make sure. Only a handful of patrons lined the bar, and he went the rest of the way inside, took a table, and waited for someone to take his order.

A strange creature, half man and half ferret, came toward him, and took his order. There wasn't much on the menu, and most of that was already gone, so he had to settle for some chili and a beer. The ferretlike man scuttled back behind the bar, spoke briefly to the bartender, then moved on into the kitchen. The bartender drew his beer, tapped the glass on the bar and shaped his right hand into a pistol, aimed at Slocum, and pulled the trigger.

Slocum retrieved his beer and was just sitting down again when the doors opened. He saw Macomb at the same time the sheriff saw him.

The big man walked to his table, kicked a chair out, and

sat down with his elbows on the table. "Slocum, been looking for you. Got to ask you a few more questions."

"Fine. I got some chili coming. You mind if I eat while we talk?"

Macomb shook his head. "Nope."

"What do you want to know?"

"You have any idea what was in them bags you told me about?"

"None whatsoever."

"Would it surprise you if I told you it was an army payroll?"

"Payroll, yes. Army, no."

Macomb seemed surprised by that. "Why not?"

"Because the canvas bags had U.S. Army stenciled on 'em. I suppose I could have guessed the payroll part, too. I didn't really think much about it. Doak really wanted those bags, though, so they must have been pretty valuable."

"Near eighteen thousand dollars valuable, in fact. You sure Doak knew about it?"

"Dead certain. He wanted the strongbox, and when the driver said there wasn't one, he started to get ugly. It was obvious he knew there was a box, and I figure that means he was expecting something particular to be in it. So he must have known about the payroll."

"But he shouldn't have."

"You ever in the army, Sheriff?"

Macomb nodded. "Twenty-eighth Ohio. Had a run-in with you rebs at Stone Mountain."

"Then you know what I mean—"

"Yeah, I know what you mean. Still, the army's sending a team here. They want to know what the hell happened, and they want to get their hands on that payroll."

"Good luck to them."

"You think Doak's long gone, do you?"

"I would be."

"If you was a stage robber, you mean." Macomb stared at him through slightly squinted eyes.

"Of course. If I was a stage robber, and I had robbed a

U.S. Army payroll, and I knew the U.S. Army was most likely not going to ignore that fact."

"You gonna have to talk to these army boys. That gal you brung in'll have to talk to 'em, too. After she talks to me again, that is."

"Fair enough."

"You know, Slocum, if I find out you're holding something back, I'll squash you like a bug. You do know that, don't you?"

"I know you'll try. But I'm not holding anything back. I told you what I saw. I told you what I did and, frankly, Sheriff, I don't much care for your insinuations."

"Don't take it personal, Slocum. You spend enough time behind this thing," he flicked the badge with a thumbnail, "you get so you don't trust your own grandma. I got a job to do. The way I see it, you can help me or not, but you better not get in my way."

Before Slocum could answer, the ferret reappeared, carrying a tray with both hands. Slocum could see the steam rising off the bowl of chili. The waiter set the tray on the table, then tilted it up for the bowl to slide off. He fished a spoon out of his pocket and set it down next to the bowl. "You need anything else?" he asked.

Slocum shook his head. "Not now, thanks."

"Two bits."

Slocum fished a quarter out of his pocket and slapped it onto the table. The ferret snatched it, then walked back to the kitchen. Slocum stuck the spoon into the chili and swirled it around until the layer of oil on the top no longer glistened. Then he let the spoon drop and cocked his head toward Macomb.

"I'll remember that, Sheriff," he said, picking up as if there had been no interruption. "I just want you to tell me one thing."

"What's that?"

"You got any particular reason to think I haven't told you the whole truth?"

Macomb shook his head. "But I got to be sure."

"You can be."

"All right. A Lieutenant Chamberlain will be here tomorrow. Meet me in my office at ten o'clock. Bring the lady."

"I'll be there."

"You better be."

9

Slocum watched the sheriff shamble toward the swinging doors. He couldn't make up his mind whether Macomb suspected him of something or was just of a suspicious turn of mind. He turned back to his chili and spooned it down without tasting it. He signaled for another beer, moved to the bar, and sat on a rough wooden stool to wash down his meal.

The bartender hovered across the scarred wood from him, sipping at a glass of water. "Sheriff giving you some problems?" he asked.

"Nothing I can't handle."

"Don't pay him no mind. He's a good man, but a little bit of a hard case. Around here, though, you can't really blame him. Used to be a time even the schoolteacher carried a gun. She don't have to do that no more. That's Macomb's doing. Course, that stage robbery wasn't calculated to mellow him none."

Slocum sipped his beer. "That happen much?"

The bartender shook his head. "Not much. Three times in the past year, though. Yesterday was the fourth. Always an army payroll. The last three was paymaster wagons, with a couple of soldiers riding shotgun. They tried the stage to

57

see would it be more secret or something, I guess. Didn't
work though, so—" He shrugged.

"Never caught the robbers?"

"Nope. Never even came close. I reckon it sticks in
Macomb's craw some, too. He don't like to lose."

"Hell, who does?"

The bartender laughed. "You got a point, there. But you
take somebody like Vance, it really gets under his saddle.
I figure whoever done it, if they was the same robbers all
four times, have about used up their luck. Having one of
them in the jailhouse won't hurt, neither."

Slocum finished his beer, pushed a quarter across the
bar, and told the barman to keep the change. He turned
and hooked his elbows over the bar to watch the street,
but it was so close to dark he couldn't really see anything.
Footsteps on the boardwalk thumped and a cowboy moved
past the doors, but that was it.

Slocum tilted his hat and walked outside. A few horses
still stood at hitching posts in front of the saloons, but there
was no traffic in the dusty street. The shops were closed.
The only business still being conducted involved alcohol.
As he walked back to the hotel, he could hear the uproar
coming from one of the more active saloons.

Blocks of light from the well-lit watering holes checkered
the street, filling wheel ruts with shadows. He crossed the
street to look inside one of the more brightly lit places,
thinking he might relax with a game of poker. But the place
was too loud. He wasn't in the mood for the steady rumble
of drunken cowboys shouting at one another to be heard.

He wasn't tired, but there was nothing he wanted to do.
Heading back to the hotel, he wondered about what the
bartender had told him. Was it possible that Doak and his
men had committed the other three robberies? Or was the
latest just a coincidence? On one level, he didn't give a
damn. Let the army take care of its own money. But events
were dragging him along, and he didn't like it.

He walked toward the edge of town, knowing it was too
early to sleep. He thought about stopping at the hotel for

Maggie, but if she was sleeping, and she probably was, it was better to let her sleep. As he drew farther away from the row of saloons, the noise slowly faded. An occasional shout and the distant tinkle of a piano were the last shreds of the ruckus.

The sky was already pitch black, hard points of light sprinkled across it. At times like this, he missed the action of the big cities. New Orleans, St. Louis, places that had something for a lonely man to do after the sun went down, things that didn't involve drinking and the risk of confrontation. He didn't care about culture. He'd seen an opera or two, been to the theater, to a concert. That sort of thing was overrated, but it was nice to know it was there.

Yuma was the other end of the world. A collection of unpainted boards doing its damnedest to hold off the sun and the sand, it could barely call itself civilized. But it did and, compared to the barren wasteland just beyond its edges, it was. It just meant that civilization wasn't all it was cracked up to be.

Slocum sat down against a rock and stared at the sky. But it just made him sad, thinking about the same stars seen from another place, in another time. Two thousand miles and as many years ago, he used to watch the night sky, listening to the sound of his mother humming as she knitted. His father would be reading, or sleeping with a book in his lap, more likely.

But all that was gone, dead as Will Callahan, and dead forever. His life had become something he had never dreamed of all those years ago. And while his life had been torn apart, he had rudely stitched it back together again, doing the best he knew how and the only thing he could. Things would never be the same again. The stars had stayed the same, but John Slocum had changed.

He scooted around the rock and leaned back, watching the few pathetic lights of Yuma wink out, one by one. The Royce Hotel was dark now. The houses, too, were black as the night itself. The only light spilled out of the bars, places full of men as lonely as he, but less aware of that loneliness, trying to drown it instead of learning to live with it.

He was starting to feel sorry for himself, and he knew it, but sometimes you had to fall all the way to the bottom of the well before you could climb out. Try to stop the fall, and all you did was bloody your hands.

Then he found himself thinking of Maggie Callahan. She led the kind of life he couldn't have, with family, friends, all those things that kept men too busy to know just how alone they really were.

But look at Maggie Callahan now, he thought. Having something means you can also lose it. He had buried the worst of his own loss years ago. It would never leave him completely, but it was a dull ache now, instead of a knife in the heart. Right now Maggie still felt the cold steel. And Slocum knew just what it felt like.

He wanted to help her, but there was nothing he could do. Her brother was not going to come back. He wondered if he could help her learn to live with that harsh fact. But he knew he couldn't. He was what he was. A woman like Maggie was different, almost another animal altogether. They couldn't really speak the same language. The words were all there, but they meant different things to each of them.

It had happened to him before, this yearning. You can't drift for too long without being drawn to someone like Maggie Callahan. But if you looked closely, it wasn't the woman herself who tempted you, it was what she represented. And what Maggie Callahan represented for John Slocum was something he could never have. His entitlement died in Georgia and had been buried there. Forever.

When the moon came up, he turned away from the town again. Watching the circle of cold light, he suppressed an involuntary shiver. It looked so close he thought he could reach out and touch it. Raising his hand, he held it cupped into a shallow bowl, letting the moon ride there as if in his palm. How real it looked. And just that easily, he thought, a man can fool himself. Even when, like Slocum, he knows better.

Getting to his feet, he turned his back on the desert, on the cold moon, and on everything he had to leave behind because it was no longer his to have.

Walking back into town, he noticed that even the racket from the saloons had died down. Lights were still on in a couple of places, but if anyone was left standing inside them, he was as silent as the desert that surrounded him on all sides. Slocum noticed a light on in the sheriff's office, low, like the wick had been turned almost all the way down on a lamp, leaving a glowing ember more than a flame.

He walked to the door, thinking to see Brady Anderson asleep at the desk, as he had been the night before. But Anderson was nowhere to be seen. The door to the cellblock was open, and he stepped into the office, his spine suddenly a column of frigid needles. Then he saw the boot on the floor at the far corner of the desk.

Something wasn't right. Drawing his Colt, he stepped to the desk and leaned over to peer behind it. Brady Anderson lay on his side, his head tilted back. A trickle of blood had run down his temple and clotted in his sparse hair. The deputy's eyes were closed. Slocum heard something from the cellblock and looked toward the open door just as a man stepped through. He had a carbine draped over one arm, and was looking back into the cellblock as he pushed through into the outer office.

He turned as Slocum brought his Colt up to his waist.

"What the hell—?"

The carbine exploded as Slocum dove behind the desk. The man bolted through the door and into the street, followed by Tom Bradley, who had a pistol in his hand.

Slocum got to his feet and raced for the door. As he started through, the carbine barked a second time. The slug tore a chunk out of the doorframe and Slocum fell backward as he instinctively ducked.

Crawling back to the doorway, he stuck his head out far enough to see the man with the carbine turn the corner. Bradley wasn't able to keep up, and Slocum brought the

Colt around and fired once. "Hold it right there, Bradley," he shouted.

The escaping prisoner cursed and threw the pistol to the ground. Slocum leaped to his feet and raced to the corner, stopped to pick up the dropped pistol, and lashed it up and under Bradley's chin. The prisoner went down in a heap, and Slocum tucked the pistol into his belt.

At the rear corner, Slocum could hear racing footsteps, but he couldn't see anyone in the darkness. Pressing himself flat against the wall, he slipped around the corner, ducked into a crouch, and sprinted along the rear wall of the sheriff's office.

The footsteps grew more distant, then vanished altogether. Slocum broke into the open and ran flat out, pausing before crossing each alley on his right. He could only guess which way the man with the carbine had gone.

A second later, he heard hoofbeats racing down the street. Slocum ran back to the nearest alleyway and raced toward the street. The hoofbeats were coming closer. He reached the mouth of the alley as the gunman went past. He fired once, but horse and rider were past the opening in a split second.

Running into the street, he saw the horse race past Bradley, who still lay unconscious in the dust. Slocum fired once, then once more, but he'd missed and he knew it.

A moment later, the gunman was gone. Racing to the fallen prisoner, he knelt beside him and hauled him to his feet. Dragging Bradley toward the open door of the sheriff's office, he heard someone shout behind him, and turned to see Macomb racing toward him, suspenders flapping over his hips and a Colt .45 in one huge hand.

"The hell is going on here, mister?"

"Sheriff," Slocum said, turning slowly toward Macomb, "somebody just tried to bust Bradley out of your jail. Did a damn good job of it, too."

"That you, Slocum?"

"Yeah, it is."

"Where's Brady?"

"Inside. Somebody busted his head and left him on the floor."

"He all right?" Macomb asked, rushing toward the open door.

"Don't know. I didn't get a chance to see. I just found him when some cowboy with a Winchester came out of the cellblock, Bradley right behind him. Took a shot at me, and I went after him."

Macomb grabbed Bradley under one arm and helped Slocum drag him back inside.

"You recognize him, Slocum?" Macomb asked.

"Didn't see him that clearly. But I don't think so. I don't think he was part of the gang that took the payroll."

"You sure about that?"

"Certain."

10

Vance Macomb slammed the cell door with a clang that could have been heard in Prescott. Shaking his head, he turned the key in the lock and backed out of the cellblock, closed the grated door, and locked it.

Slocum was squatting alongside the sheriff's chair, trying to get Brady Anderson to say something besides "Oh, my damn head." When the deputy noticed the sheriff, he slid down in the chair a couple of inches, but there was no place for him to hide.

Slocum straightened, then moved toward the door.

"Where the hell you goin', Slocum?" Macomb snapped. "You might as well hear this."

Slocum nodded. "Whatever you say, Sheriff."

Turning to the deputy, Macomb said, "Brady, what the hell happened here?"

The deputy moaned, then reached gingerly to stroke the sizable lump above his left temple. "I don't know, Sheriff."

"Who was that bastard?"

"Said he was lookin' for somebody. Asked did I know where to find him."

"Who was he lookin' for?"

Anderson cocked a thumb over his shoulder. "Him. Bradley. So I told him we had him inside. He asked could he see him and I said I didn't know. He walked to the door, there, and peeked through the grate, said something like 'Howdy, Tommy.' I got up to chase him away, and the next thing I know he slugged me on the ear. I don't know what he hit me with, but it done the trick, I guess."

Macomb made a disgusted sound and shook his head. "Damn it, Brady. He almost sprung that man. You got to pay more attention. I keep tellin' you that. Was you sleeping again?"

Anderson looked to Slocum for support, but Slocum said nothing. Brady was on his own, and he didn't quite know how to cope with the responsibility. "I guess I was, Vance. I'm awful sorry."

"Sorry don't feed the dog, Brady. Sumbitch coulda killed you, he wanted to, you know that?"

"Yes, sir, I do."

"What would I tell Martha, if that was to happen? You want me to have to tell your widow you got yourself shot because you were too damn lazy to keep your eyes open?"

"No, Vance."

"He tell you his name?" Slocum asked.

Macomb looked sharply at Slocum, but it was a good question, and he kept his mouth shut.

The deputy shook his head. "No, he didn't tell me nothing, except what I already told you he said. That was all. There wasn't all that much time between when he come in and when he slugged me."

"You ever seen him before, Brady?" Macomb asked.

"No, sir, never did. Don't even know if I could recognize him if I seen him again. The light was down kinda low and all. It was kinda dark. I guess that's how come he was able to get at me like that."

"Bullshit, Brady. He was able to get at you because you don't pay attention. You never do. This time it almost got you killed and almost cost us a murder suspect. You're lucky Slocum, here, happened along, or I'd have to fire your ass for incompetence, Brady."

Anderson sank deeper into the chair. "I'm sorry, Vance. I swear to God, it won't happen again."

"Damn right it won't. You go along home. I'll talk to you tomorrow. But you better be here at ten sharp. That damn lieutenant's gonna be here. I'm gonna need all the help I can get when I'm through with him."

"You don't want me to stay on tonight?"

Macomb almost lost it then. Slocum was certain he would. But the sheriff swallowed his anger and walked to the front door. Taking a deep breath and letting it out in a long, slow, exasperated hiss, he shook his head as he turned. "No, Brady, I think you already done enough work for tonight. You go on home and have Martha see to your head."

Anderson got up quickly. It was obvious to Slocum that the deputy felt he'd gotten a reprieve he hadn't expected. He was grateful, and not about to hang around long enough for Macomb to change his mind. He clapped his hat on his head, groaned at the sudden stab of pain from the lump on his head, and shuffled out the door.

When Anderson was gone, Macomb dropped into the big leather chair behind his desk. "That sumbitch hasn't got the sense he was born with, Slocum. And I guess I'm obliged to you. You hadn't come along when you did, they might have hurt him worse, maybe killed him. I thank you for helping out."

"No thanks necessary, Sheriff. I just wish I knew what the hell was going on around here."

"You and me both, Slocum. You and me both. And I don't expect the army's gonna tell us much, neither. They're a closemouthed bunch of bastards. They like to come in and run the show, but they don't want to tell you what the show is. I don't mind tellin' you, it makes me madder'n hell to take that spit and polish guff. But I got to go along with 'em as best I can."

"You don't mind, Sheriff, I think I'll move along. I could use a little shut-eye. Unless you want me to hang around here with you."

"That won't be necessary. They won't be stupid enough to try the same thing twice in one night. When they come back, if they do, they'll have plenty of help. But it won't be tonight. I'll handle things here. Starting tomorrow, I'm gonna have to deputize a few men and run double guard shifts until the trial."

"You're sure you don't need me?"

"I'm sure, but I'm obliged for the offer."

"Good night, Sheriff," Slocum said, getting out of the chair.

"Night."

As Slocum stepped to the door, the sheriff added, "And Slocum, thanks for your help tonight. I guess I owe you an apology. I'm sorry if I rubbed you the wrong way, but—"

"Forget it, Sheriff."

"No, sir, I don't forget things like that. I owe you one. And I always pay what I owe."

"See you in the morning."

Slocum walked back to the hotel, even more concerned than when he'd left it. He started to think about the man who'd been in his room, wondering if it was the same man who'd been to the jailhouse. And whether it would be better if he were. He was beginning to suspect that Doak had enlisted some reinforcements. And he knew that Bradley was in some danger. If they couldn't break him out, there was the possibility they might try to kill him. They had, after all, left him behind, either thinking him dead or not giving a damn. But now that they knew he was in custody, he was a threat to Doak and the others, a threat they would not likely ignore.

At the hotel, Slocum stopped to look up the street. He could see a bright block of light from the sheriff's office. Macomb was likely going to stay up all night. Two saloons were still open, but even as Slocum stood there in front of the glass doors, a man appeared on the walk in front of one of them, closed and locked the doors, and stepped out of sight into the shadows.

There was nothing to be gained standing there, so he went on inside and climbed the stairs. His feet felt as if they were weighted with lead, and the climb to the second floor was an effort. As he turned the corner to his room, he broke into a brisk walk. He wanted more than anything to climb into bed and sleep. A week would be fine, a month would be better.

As he reached his room and inserted the key, he heard a latch turn somewhere to his right. He opened his door and waited. A door opened. In the dim light, he couldn't tell which one.

"Slocum? Is that you?"

"Miss Callahan?" He left his door open and moved back down the hall. Maggie was in her doorway. The room behind her was barely lit.

"Can I talk to you?" she asked.

Slocum nodded.

She stepped aside and gestured for him to come in. When he moved past her, she closed the door, muffling the latch with the palm of her hand.

"Anything wrong?" he asked.

Her voice was even huskier, probably with recent sleep. "No. I don't know. Maybe."

"What's the matter?"

He turned to look at her then, and realized her legs were bare. She seemed to be wearing only a blue denim shirt. She hugged herself tightly, and her body shook with a shiver that had nothing to do with the temperature.

"I'm frightened," she said. "I came to your room but you weren't there. I thought you'd left."

"Why would I do that?"

"Why should you stay?"

"I'm a witness. The sheriff told me to stay."

She let her arms fall. "Slocum, you and I both know that you don't give a damn what the sheriff says. Isn't that so?"

He didn't answer right away. She took his silence as agreement. "See?"

"You want me to ask the sheriff for a guard for you?"

"No. That's not what I want."

He shook his head. "All right."

"Can you stay with me tonight? I don't mean—I just—I guess I'd feel better, having someone here with me."

"And I'm as good as any, is that it?"

"Not exactly. But I feel I can trust you."

"A moment ago you said you thought I'd left. Now you say you trust me. Which is it, Miss Callahan?"

"Both, I guess. I'm sorry. Maybe you shouldn't stay."

"It's all right. If you'll feel safer, I'll stay. Just let me get a couple of things from my room."

"Do you have to?" She laughed then. "I'm sorry. You must think I'm a nuisance."

"I'm starting to, yes."

"I suppose I don't blame you."

"That's very kind of you, ma'am."

"Don't make fun of me, Slocum. I don't need that. Especially not now."

He walked to the door and opened it. "I'll be right back," he said, and stepped into the hall. From his room he gathered some blankets and a pillow, bundled them in his arms, and walked back to Maggie's room. She took the key from his outstretched hand and went to lock his room.

He had already arranged his bedroll on the floor by the time she returned. Sitting on the floor, he pulled off his boots. His unbuckled gun belt was coiled right beside his pillow. She walked to the bed and sat down.

He hadn't realized how muscular she was, but the long legs not five feet away were impossible to ignore. She noticed his appraisal, but said nothing.

The lamp was on a small dresser beside his makeshift mattress. He reached up to turn down the wick.

"Don't do that," she said. "I don't want it to be dark." She lay back on the bed. It was a warm night, and she didn't bother with a blanket. She crossed her legs and closed her eyes.

For a long time, Slocum listened to her breathing. Once, he opened his eyes to look at her. She was watching him. She smiled and closed her eyes. "Good night, Mr. Slocum," she said.

11

Slocum was awake before the sun came up. He lay there on his stomach, his head half buried in the pillow. Aware of the sun, he felt its heat in a narrow band across his back where it stabbed through the curtains.

He had slept only sporadically. There were too many questions for him to have slept well. And knowing that Maggie Callahan was less than a body's length away hadn't made it any easier. He heard her stirring and finally sat up. She was still lying there, those long legs stretched out to their full length. He couldn't tell whether she was awake or not.

He got up on his knees and gathered his bedroll into a mound. Without saying anything, he walked to the door. He closed it softly, walked to his own room, and opened the door. Inside, he made ready to shave, but paid little attention as he scraped at several days' growth. His bath would have to wait until the afternoon.

When he was finished trying to make himself look civilized, if not presentable, he wiped the last curls of shaving soap from his cheeks and under his chin, dressed, and went down for breakfast.

He stretched the meal out as long as he could, then

walked down to the livery stable to check on the chestnut. His pocket watch showed him he still had two hours before Lieutenant Walter Chamberlain was scheduled to arrive. He thought about stopping by the sheriff's office, but decided to pass on it. He'd spent enough time there already in the last few days. Yuma wasn't much, but he thought there ought to be more to it than a building full of iron cages.

He walked back to the hotel and went up to his room. There was a note under his door. It was from Maggie, telling him she had gone to breakfast without him. He could almost hear the scolding tone of it, as if it had been dictated by an angry schoolteacher. He thought perhaps he had been rude, but it hadn't been his intention. If Maggie wanted to take offense, that was her prerogative.

He lay on his bed, still stripped of its blankets, which lay in a heap in a corner of the room. The time passed slowly, ticked off second by second by an ugly Swiss clock high on one wall. At nine thirty, he knew there was no point in delaying any longer. He'd be early at Sheriff Macomb's, but he'd run out of ways to kill time.

The street was full of activity when he descended to the lobby for the second time that morning. The sun was already noontime bright. Unlike the past couple of days, there was no breeze. The motionless air filled the lobby, feeling like a thick, invisible blanket. He felt as if he couldn't breathe normally as he stepped out into the street.

Slocum glanced toward the sheriff's office, where he saw three horses tied off at the rail. The nearest one sported a typical U.S. Cavalry saddle blanket. So, he thought, the lieutenant has already arrived. Maybe they could get things out of the way sooner than planned.

He broke into a swift walk, only to stop in his tracks when Maggie Callahan called after him. He turned to see her hurrying toward him, her long legs encased in faded denim. For the first time, he realized there wasn't a straight line on her body. Everything took long, leisurely detours, curving this way and that, on the way from head to foot. Stripped of the smothering layers of petticoats and gingham, she looked like a different woman, and he saw just how attractive she was.

She caught up to him, scowled, and said, "I thought we'd have breakfast together."

"I couldn't sleep," he said.

"I know."

"You didn't seem to have any trouble."

"I had more than you think, Mr. Slocum. But self-discipline is something I have worked long and hard to cultivate. Unfortunately, I seem to have succeeded." The smile she gave him could have meant a dozen things, and he didn't dare think about any of them.

"We better go see Sheriff Macomb," he said.

"I hope he's more pleasant than usual."

Slocum turned without responding. Well before they reached the office, Slocum could hear raised voices. As they drew closer, the words began to become intelligible. By the time he reached the doorway, it was obvious Macomb and Lieutenant Chamberlain did not see eye to eye.

Slocum stepped into the office, pausing in mid-stride for a split second to rap his knuckles on the open door. Ralph Winslow and Tim Cartwright stood in one corner, listening to the argument. The lieutenant, a tall, thin man with long blond hair, turned to frown at the intruder.

"We're busy," he snapped, the words chopped into pieces by his large buckteeth. To try and conceal them, he sported a thick yellow mustache, which served only to call attention to his hatchetlike nose. His eyes were blue and small, too close together, and at the moment, more than a little agitated.

"I'm supposed to be here," Slocum said, unimpressed by the lieutenant's imperious manner.

"Who are you?"

"That's Slocum, the man I was telling you about."

Chamberlain nodded. "I see. Well, then, Mr. Slocum, perhaps you can tell me why you're late."

"Hey, listen to me, Lieutenant. I'm not in your army. I'm here because the sheriff asked me to cooperate, not because

I've been impressed into service."

"Reb, are you?"

"The war's over, Lieutenant. Haven't you heard? And you won, so why don't you just relax?"

"I don't like your attitude, Slocum."

"Compared to you, Chamberlain, I don't even *have* an attitude." He looked at Macomb. "Sheriff, I'll come back later."

"The hell you will," Chamberlain barked, drawing his side arm. "You'll stay right here, mister, until I tell you otherwise."

"What's this all about, Sheriff?" Slocum demanded, ignoring the lieutenant again.

Macomb shrugged. "Just try to get through it. You'll have to put up with the toy soldier," he said.

Chamberlain glared at him, but didn't say anything. If he had the sense that he was now outnumbered, he made no outward sign. Staring past Slocum, he asked, "Who's the woman? What's she doing here?"

Maggie stepped forward, squeezing Slocum's arm as she moved him to one side. "Margaret Callahan, Lieutenant," she said. "And I'm here for the same reason Mr. Slocum is. Because the sheriff asked us to cooperate with you. And it might be nice if you'd show a little appreciation."

"I don't have time for courtesy, ma'am. I have a robbery to investigate."

"And I have a brother to bury. We all have our pressing obligations, Lieutenant Chamberlain. That doesn't mean we have to be rude."

Chamberlain grunted. "Let's get on with it then, shall we?"

He started to ask questions, and he took them all over the same ground one by one and then as a group. When he was through interrogating them, very little light had been shed, but more than a little heat had been generated. Slocum was on the verge of taking a swing at him, and only a sharp glare from Macomb prevented him from doing so.

When he was finished with his grilling, Chamberlain

said, "I understand there will be a trial next week for the one man Johnny Reb, here, captured. Since you'll all be here at least through the trial, I'd appreciate it if you'd let the sheriff know anything you might remember that you haven't already told me now."

"I'm surprised you can appreciate anything at all," Maggie mumbled. It was just loud enough for them all to hear. Chamberlain started to say something, but Macomb saved him.

"Don't worry about it, Lieutenant, everybody wants to get this mess cleared up. Nobody more'n me."

Chamberlain left without another word. When he was gone, Slocum turned to the sheriff. "That pompous bastard couldn't find his ass with both hands. How in hell they won the war is beyond me."

Macomb laughed. "They had me, too, Slocum. Remember that."

Ralph Winslow was less critical. He had been curiously subdued during the questioning. His voice was a little stronger now, but not much. "The man's just trying to do his job, after all. And you didn't have to give him such a hard time, Slocum."

"I didn't give him half the hard time I wanted to, Winslow. Maybe you should just mind your own business."

Winslow reached out to take Maggie by the arm. "I'm not sure you ought to have anything to do with this man. It wouldn't surprise me if he knew more about that robbery than he's told us."

"Ralph, mind your own business."

"Maggie, I think Will would agree. He wouldn't—"

"Ralph, Will thought you were a bit of a blowhard. I'm beginning to think he was too generous by half."

Winslow dropped his hand from Maggie's arm. He moved toward the door, looked back once, then stepped out onto the boardwalk. Tim Cartwright excused himself and followed the chubby accountant.

Slocum and Maggie followed him out. Slocum heard the crack, and saw Cartwright stagger. It took a second to register. A rifle, somewhere to the left, and up.

He shoved Maggie back into the sheriff's office and drew his Colt as Cartwright fell to one knee. Another shot slammed into the wall, just above Slocum's head. He dove into the street, using Cartwright as a springboard and shoving the kid back and to the walkway at the same instant.

Winslow scurried past him and stumbled back into the sheriff's office.

Two more shots rang out, both chewing at the dirt inches from Slocum's rolling body. He scurried toward the army horses and got to his feet, using them for cover. He saw the brim of a hat behind a false wall over the Yuma Hotel.

Snatching a Springfield repeater from the boot on one of the cavalry mounts, he pumped a shell into the chamber, slipped off the safety, and sighted in on the false wall.

The hat brim was gone. Over to the left, another man suddenly appeared, sighting down a rifle barrel just as Slocum glimpsed him out of the corner of his eye.

Swinging the borrowed rifle to the left, he drew a bead six inches below the head. Squeezing the trigger, he worked the lever, chambered another round, and fired a second time.

He could see two holes in the false wall, one three inches below and two to the left of the other. He waited for another target to present itself, but nothing happened. It was suddenly perfectly quiet.

"You all right, Slocum?" Macomb called.

"All right, Sheriff."

"You get him?"

"I don't know. There were two, I think, maybe more. How's the kid?"

He turned, then, and looked toward Tim Cartwright, who lay flat on his back, a couple of feet to the left of the doorway. There was a pool of blood on the weathered wood. And two holes in Tim's chest.

Macomb ran past him and down an alley to get behind the hotel and up to the roof. Maggie sat beside the kid and lifted his head into her lap. He wasn't breathing. He wasn't going to make it, Slocum thought. And where the hell was Chamberlain while all this was going on? he wondered.

He saw Macomb at the back of the alley. "Nothing—" he shouted. "You missed 'em."

But missed who? Slocum asked himself.

12

Slocum was eating in the hotel dining room when Maggie Callahan came in. She spotted him immediately and walked toward his table. "Do you mind if I join you?" she asked.

He shook his head.

"Not talking?"

"I generally don't," he said.

She sat down, and Slocum raised his hand to catch a waiter's eye. The place was small, but tried hard, and the food wasn't bad. The waiter handed her a small hand-lettered menu. She glanced at it, chose a steak, and the waiter disappeared. Looking at Slocum, then, she said, "One thing I've learned out here is that it's difficult to ruin steak."

"Don't be too sure of that," Slocum replied.

She laughed, but it died quickly. "What do you think of our Lieutenant Chamberlain?" she asked.

"Not in polite company."

"Don't be too sure of that," she said. He looked up sharply. "Turnabout, Mr. Slocum. Besides, I really do want to know."

"What did you think?"

"I think he's the kind of rude young man woodsheds were made for. At least, that's what my father said they were

78

for. In this particular instance, I don't think I'd disagree with him."

"That'll do."

"No, it won't. What did you think, honestly?"

Slocum rubbed his fingers over his lips. It looked almost as if he were trying to wipe away the first words that occurred to him. "I think he needs to be taught some manners. But I think it's more than that. I think he's getting at something, almost like he knows something we don't know, or something he thinks we don't know. But he isn't sure, so he pushes. It's more like he wants to know how much we know, instead of *what* we know."

Maggie reached across the table and took the lone water tumbler. Before raising it to her lips, she asked, "Do you mind?"

When he shook his head, she took a sip and set the glass back where it had been. "What do you think he's worried about, John?"

Slocum noticed the informality, but tried not to show it. "I wish I knew. But something tells me I will, before too long. Whatever it is, he's determined to push this thing as far as he can."

"Did you notice how Ralph was trying to stay on his good side?"

"Yeah. I don't know what to make of that."

"You know Ralph was here conducting an audit of some kind, don't you?"

"No. But why should that make a difference?"

"I don't know. I don't even know who it was for. I just think it does make a difference, somehow. It certainly seemed like it. And it was strange, the way he acted when that young man was killed this afternoon. That was so terrible, but for Ralph it seemed like something more than that."

"You must think the Southwest is a pretty violent place."

"Don't you?"

Slocum didn't answer right away. Maggie noticed his reluctance. "You don't have to answer, if you don't want to. I know I'm used to a tamer world. But—"

"No. You're right. It is violent. But that will change someday."

"Will we live to see that day, you and I, John?"

"Probably not both of us, no."

They lapsed into silence. Slocum had more or less lost his appetite. When Maggie's food was delivered, she toyed with it awhile. Finally, laying her fork and knife down, she said, "I guess I'm not really hungry."

Slocum smiled distantly. "Not surprising," he said.

He stood up and left money on the table to pay for both meals. He caught the waiter's eye, indicated the table, and helped Maggie out of her chair.

"So gallant," she said.

"Not hardly."

"Yes, you are. Don't be so hard on yourself."

"If I'm not, who will be?"

"A wife, probably."

Slocum snorted outright at that. "No, Miss Callahan, I really don't think so."

He moved toward the door, and she followed him. Out on the walk, he looked up at the sky. "Looks like rain," he said.

"Where are you going now?"

"Thought I'd take a walk."

"Do you mind if I come along?"

"I'd rather you not."

She looked hurt, and he hadn't meant for that to happen.

"Nothing personal. I just need a little time to myself."

"Maybe you have too much of that as it is."

Slocum shrugged. "Maybe—"

"Well, I won't impose on you, then. Good night." Her tone was cool now, almost formal. He watched her enter the hotel lobby. On the stairs, she turned to look back at the front door. He was still watching, but she made no sign that it meant anything to her.

When Maggie was out of sight at the top of the stairs, he

walked down to the sheriff's office. Macomb wasn't there, but Brady Anderson was.

"Mr. Slocum," he said. "Come to see if I'm awake, did you?"

Slocum laughed. "Brady, I think you probably learned your lesson."

"You can say that again. Want to look in on the prisoner?"

Slocum shook his head. "Sheriff not here?"

"He's off somewhere with that Lieutenant Chamberlain. How he can stand the company, I don't know."

"You like him, too, huh?"

"What's to like? We already got more snakes, scorpions, and spiders than we need. Givin' one a commission don't seem to make much sense to me."

"Well, thanks. Tell him I was by, would you?"

"Sure will."

He headed toward the edge of town. He didn't really have any particular place to go, but he didn't relish the thought of being cooped up in his room so early. He was beginning to feel like a prisoner, himself. It didn't matter that he wasn't behind bars. He still couldn't go where he wanted to go, when he wanted to. Maybe he should just ride on, leave the mess behind him. It wasn't his mess, anyway. Let somebody else clean it up.

Then he thought of Macomb, who had changed his tune a little. They sure weren't friends, but he had told the sheriff he'd be there for the trial. He always kept his word, even when he wished he hadn't given it. This time shouldn't be any different.

And, of course, there was Maggie Callahan. The funeral for Will was the following morning. It wouldn't be right to leave her alone. Not yet. And the way she looked at him did something funny to his spine, made him shiver somehow. He didn't know why, and didn't really want to think about it. Better to just pretend it didn't happen.

Just a few days, that's all he had left in this goddamned outhouse of a town. He could handle that, he thought.

Then, as if he had been arguing with himself and lost, he shrugged, turned back toward the hotel, and kicked at the dusty street.

Back at the hotel, the clerk watched him out of the corner of his eye. Slocum shook his head, fed up with Yuma and everyone in it. As he ground the key in the lock of his room, Maggie opened her door.

"John, can I talk to you?" she asked. He turned, but didn't see her. Moving toward the doorway to her room, he reached it and stopped. The room was dark, and Maggie was nowhere to be seen.

"Anything wrong?"

"No."

He stepped inside, and the door closed behind him. He heard the latch click and turned toward the sound. Arms closed around his neck, and he reached out instinctively for his assailant. His fingers found nothing but skin and more skin.

Maggie's voice was in his ear as she pressed up against him. He let his hands rest on her back, feeling the smoothness of skin, the firmness beneath it. She pushed against him, forcing him backward to keep from stumbling.

"What's going on?" he asked, confused.

"What do you think is going on, Mr. Slocum?"

The backs of his knees hit the bed and her body propelled him over and down. He felt fingers claw at his chest as the buttons of his shirt came away. Then the weight of her breasts flattened against his naked chest. Her nipples were hard, and she radiated a kind of heat so different from the cool skin of her back.

Her breath whispered against his face, then her lips pressed his. Her insistent tongue found its way into his mouth, and his hands slipped lower, tracing the fullness of her ass. He rose on one hip as she slid off to lay beside him. Leaning over her, he felt her hand slide down his chest and slip into his dungarees. She found what she was looking for.

He fumbled with his buttons while she stroked him. When the jeans were open, she let go of him and got on her knees, tugging the pants down and off. He reached for her again, felt the weight of her as she straddled him. Erect against her stomach, he felt the flutter of her fingers as she stroked him to a rocklike hardness. He could hear the soft rustle of her fingertips in the lush thatch between her legs.

Her weight lifted, and he was swallowed by something warm and wet. Maggie moaned, and he felt her body shudder as she lowered herself down onto him. She swiveled her hips to drive him even deeper, then leaned over until her nipples brushed the tight curls on his chest. The slight sway of them sent a shiver up his spine.

Her hips began to move and he picked up her rhythm; slow, almost cautious at first, she made each shuddering withdrawal seem as if it would be the last. Slowly picking up speed, she slipped her arms beneath him, pressing her breasts flat as he started to buck. She moaned again, grinding her hips against his. Stroking her back, he let his fingers trace her spine, stopping at each bone for a moment, then moving on to the beginning of the cleft, where he let his hands lie still, the coolness of her bottom almost perfect under them.

Her breath grew sharp as she rose and fell. They didn't speak. The room was full only of their breathing and the murmur of her wetness. Her teeth nicked his shoulder, nipping at the skin a moment. She licked him then, her hot tongue tracing the curve of his throat until it slid into his waiting mouth like a living flame.

He grabbed her hips now and held her, taming her rhythm until it was steady and he could match her rise and fall. In tune, he lifted her as he backed away, then lowered her as he raised his hips, again, a little faster, until she began to shudder, and her breath was shattered into little cries. She raised up off him then, and in the darkness he couldn't see her at all, only feel the weight of her as she pressed down harder, pulling him deeper inside, then shivered and fell on him with one final moan.

"I lied," she muttered.

"What?"

"I said, I lied. There was something wrong. But it's all right now."

"You sure?"

"Not quite," she whispered.

13

Slocum awoke with Maggie's legs tangled in his. One arm draped across his chest and pinned him to the mattress. He tried to extricate himself without waking her. Part of him wanted to stay, but in his mind's eye he kept seeing the smirk of the desk clerk telling him Maggie wanted to see him, and he couldn't bring himself to stay.

It took ten minutes of careful maneuvering to untangle their bodies, but he finally managed to get off the bed. He stood there in the dark, listening to her breathe. The moon coming through the curtains traced a pattern of shadowy snowflakes on the floor. As he moved away from the bed, the shadows fell over his feet. He stopped for a moment and realized the dark lines looked like a tracery of veins in the feet of an old man.

And Maggie Callahan made him feel just like that, a man old before his time. He felt as if the best part of his life was behind him. He hated that melancholy streak in himself, but he knew he had to accept it, as he had learned to accept so much else. Women like Maggie were rare. That one of them could feel something for him, even momentary lust, was something he had learned to accept, but not to hope for. And he never permitted himself to hope that it would be anything *but* momentary.

Stepping to the window, he pulled the heavy drapes and the lace curtain aside and let the light flood the room. Looking at Maggie, lying on her back, the full breasts defying gravity, their nipples still erect from the cool night air, she looked as if she had been cast from something like silver, not as shiny as that precious metal, but more durable.

One leg, bent at the knee, was outlined with shadow where the muscles of her calf were drawn taut. The smooth expanse of her stomach seemed to reflect a little of the light as her breathing caused it to rise and fall. She was more than pretty. She was beautiful, but without the arrogance he had come to expect from such a woman.

But there was no point in standing there like an idiot, wishing for something he knew could never be. With a twinge of regret, he let the curtain fall, then the drape, and Maggie Callahan sank back into shadow, the same way she would, in a few short days, sink into the past.

Gathering his clothes, he moved into a corner of the room and slipped into his pants. He buckled the gun belt and draped it over one shoulder. Clutching his shirt and boots in one hand, he stepped to the door and slowly turned the latch, trying not to wake her.

The latch clicked, and he heard her stir. The sound of her skin on the sheet was like unexpected thunder. He thought for a moment she was awake, going to say something that would make it impossible for him to leave. But she took a deep breath, released it with a sigh, then the silence returned.

He closed the door carefully, then walked to his own room. Setting the boots on the floor, he fished his key out of his pocket and opened the door. Once the door closed behind him, he took a deep breath. Lying on his own bed, he kept the gun belt by his side. He listened to the night for a long time. Far in the distance, the yip of a coyote echoed once or twice, then even the night fell quiet.

It was nearly dawn when he heard the noise on the balcony. At first, he wasn't sure. He'd been hearing so much, or thinking he had, for two days. There was a limit to how much a man ought to worry. But this time he couldn't convince himself he'd imagined it.

He sat up and leaned toward the open window. Once more, he heard it. A creak, wood stressed, like an old tree under the pressure of a high wind. Slocum moved to the window. It was still dark, but the sun would be up in half an hour. He knew, almost without thinking, that it was the perfect time. Still dark, the very bottom of the night, when even sentries fell asleep leaning on their rifles.

Slocum crouched by the window and bunched the lace in one hand. He pulled it to one side and looped it through the drapery tieback. Looking straight ahead, all he could see was the desert landscape, still painted a pale gray by the declining moon.

He wanted to climb out onto the balcony, but didn't want to risk losing the slight edge surprise would give him. He heard another creak. It was coming from the far end of the balcony, where the stairs descended to the alley behind the hotel.

Leaning out, he saw no one, but knew there was someone on the stairway. There wasn't enough noise for him to tell how many—one, two, maybe even three. He wished Maggie were with him, and even as the thought crossed his mind, he pictured her lying there on the bed, naked, vulnerable, and alone.

Her window, too, was open. He debated going to her door, but the noise might alarm whoever was climbing to the balcony. Better to wait, get the drop on him—or them—and maybe finally get the leverage to open the jar, see what was inside it.

Slocum moved silently back to the bed and retrieved his gun belt. He thought about letting it sit on the floor, but realized that he might need it. In case he had to move quickly, he didn't need another thing to think about. Backing away from the window a couple of steps, he buckled the gun belt on, then unholstered the Colt.

Kneeling again by the sill, he brought his head close to the window. The sound changed now. Instead of the creak of the stairs, he heard the scrape of leather soles on rough wood. This was no drunken salesman sneaking in the back way.

The gun felt cold in his hand, but his palm was sweating. The scraping stopped, tempting him to look out along the balcony, but he had waited this long; he would just have to rein himself in—and wait.

The noise started again, growing just a little louder as the men approached. He thought there were two now, but couldn't be sure. A whisper hissed for a split second, then was cut off, as if a hand had been clapped over careless lips. The footsteps resumed. He wished he could tell how close, but the sound was too feeble for him to be certain.

Then a sash creaked as it was moved in its channel. It sounded close. Slocum stuck his head out into the darkness. He could see the man then, one knee hooked through Maggie's window. Beyond him, another man crouched by the railing.

Slocum's pistol felt heavy as he shifted it to his left hand.

"That'll be about far enough, gents," he hissed.

A bullet slammed into the windowsill just past his shoulder. He saw the flash at the same instant and heard the crack, sounding louder than it was, of the discharge.

A woman, certainly Maggie, screamed as Slocum pulled the trigger once, then again.

A second shot chipped at the window frame as the nearer man fell backward, his right leg still hooked over the sill of Maggie's window. Slocum followed him in the awkward arc and fired a third time.

Someone groaned, and footsteps pounded hollowly on the boards. Tumbling through the window, Slocum nearly went through the rickety railing and down into the alley. The man still had his foot on the sill and it fell with a thump as he twisted in pain and tried to get to his feet. He seemed aware of Slocum only then. In the pale moonlight, Slocum saw the glint of the Colt in the man's hand and fired again.

The raised Colt slipped from the man's hand, fell to the boards, then slid off and landed on the dirt below. Slocum scrambled past the wounded man and raced down the balcony. Already, the second man was on the stairs. It sounded as if he was taking them two at a time. No longer concerned with noise, he leaped the last few steps, just as Slocum reached the head of the stairs. He turned and fired, forcing Slocum to duck back. Slocum bumped the wall of the building and lost his grip on the Navy. Bending to recover it, he heard another gunshot below him.

Footsteps pounded on the dry ground and Slocum started down the steps. Six feet off the ground, he jumped, let bent knees absorb the shock, then scrambled along the alley. He could see the dull gray outline running full tilt until it turned a corner and was gone.

The thought of Maggie arrested him in mid-stride, and he turned and ran back to the stairs. Taking them two at a time, he reached the balcony and raced along it as people ducked their heads back in, one after another. The wounded man still lay on the balcony, one arm dangling out over the edge. Slocum knelt beside him, leaning close to peer into his face. But it was no one he had seen before.

Feeling for the man's throat, he tried to find a pulse. But there was none. Someone shouted from two or three rooms down. Slocum heard the click of a hammer being cocked. "Get the sheriff," he shouted, then moved to the window.

"Maggie, are you all right?"

"Slocum?"

"Yes."

She threw herself at him, almost knocking him down. "Thank God," she whispered. "I was scared to death."

"With reason," he said. "They were trying to break into your room."

"I heard the gunfire. The first shot woke me up, and I didn't know what was happening."

He stroked her hair for a moment, then let his hand slide down over the thick curls to her back. Only then did he remember she was naked.

He let his hand fall, but she continued to cling to him.

"I didn't know—"

The pounding on the door was so sudden, it startled them both.

"Open up in there!"

"That's the sheriff," Slocum said.

"I have to get dressed," she whispered. Then, turning toward the door, which continued to rattle under a heavy fist, she shouted, "Just a minute."

Slocum waited while she slipped on a pair of dungarees and a shirt. She fumbled with the lamp, got it lit, then whispered, "All right."

Slocum walked to the door and opened it. Macomb stood there with a drawn Colt. "You all right, Slocum? Miss Callahan all right?"

Slocum backed away from the door to let the sheriff in. Behind the lawman, a half dozen curious residents crowded around the open doorway.

Macomb turned to the hallway. "Go on home, folks. Everything's under control." Without ceremony, he slammed the door. "Nothing but a flock of goddamned buzzards," he muttered, "the whole pack of 'em."

Tugging on one ear, he holstered his pistol. "Now, what in hell is going on here?"

Slocum jerked a thumb toward the window. Walking over to grab the lamp, he moved to the window and pulled the curtains aside. "See for yourself," he said, holding the lamp high enough to let its light illuminate the body on the balcony.

Macomb leaned out the window. "Who's that? He one of 'em?"

Slocum shook his head. "Never saw him before, Sheriff."

Macomb looked at Maggie. "You ever seen him before, Miss Callahan?"

"I haven't seen him yet, Sheriff."

"Then you better have a look, see do you know him. I know it ain't easy, but you got to do it."

Maggie sighed and looked at Slocum. He remained quiet, and she took a couple of tentative steps. Macomb moved aside, and she stood there, staring out into the night. In the orange light, she could see the man's face clearly. She looked a long time. Slocum wondered what was going through her head. When she turned away, she said, "No. I've never seen him."

"You sure?"

"Sheriff, the men you are looking for killed my brother. I was there. I saw it *happen*. Do you really think I wouldn't recognize one of those animals if I saw him again?"

"No, ma'am, I suppose not."

14

The morning of the funeral was the hottest day yet. Slocum was up early, and he was not looking forward to the service. He walked to the sheriff's office, feeling the sun pressing down on him like an invisible flatiron. Vance Macomb was sitting at his desk, and Ralph Winslow sat in a chair in a corner. It looked almost as if the fat accountant were trying to get as far away from the lawman as possible without actually leaving the office.

Macomb looked up when Slocum entered.

"You wanted to see me, Sheriff?" Slocum said.

Macomb nodded. "That I do, Mr. Slocum. That I do. Seems like we got us a little problem, here, and I was wondering if you could help me out."

"What kind of problem?"

Macomb stabbed one blunt finger at the fat man in the corner. "That kind of problem."

Winslow had his hands in his lap, the fingers intertwined. His eyes darted nervously around the office, as if he were looking for someplace to hide. Slocum said hello, but Winslow didn't respond.

Slocum looked back to the sheriff, who had his eyebrows raised. Macomb shrugged. "Seems like Mr. Winslow don't remember what he remembered yesterday. Seems he either misremembered or forgot, or I don't know what all. Ain't that right, Mr. Winslow?"

"I told you what I told you, Sheriff."

"Which time would that be, Mr. Winslow? The first or the second time? Because what you told me this morning sure ain't what you told me the first time we talked about it."

"That's what happened. What I told you."

"This morning?"

Winslow's flabby lips flapped, but no sound came out of his mouth. When he realized Macomb was waiting for an answer, he nodded his head. The layered jowls shuddered under his chin with the motion.

Slocum finally interrupted. "What's this all about, Sheriff?"

"What this is about, Mr. Slocum, is that Mr. Winslow now tells me he didn't see anybody, not clear enough so's he could identify 'em, anyhow. Says he was too scared, and that he stayed in the coach until it was all over."

"That's bullshit!" Slocum said. "We all got out of the coach at gunpoint. He was standing—"

Macomb raised a hand to calm him down. "That's not what he recollects now. According to Mr. Winslow, you and Will Callahan was the only ones to see what happened. He says Miss Callahan was in the stage the whole time. He don't even know whether Will Callahan was shot or stabbed to death." The sheriff glanced at Winslow. "Ain't that right, Mr. Winslow?"

"I didn't see anything, Sheriff. I swear it."

"That wouldn't have anything to do with what happened to Timmy Cartwright, would it?" Macomb asked.

"Who?"

The sheriff threw up his hands. "Seems like you forgot just about everything, Winslow."

"I didn't forget. I just was upset. I don't know what I told you the other day. It doesn't matter. What I'm telling you now is what happened."

"What happened, Winslow?" Slocum asked. "Somebody get to you? Is somebody threatening you?"

Winslow barely mumbled the answer. "No, nothing like that."

"What, then? You don't expect Miss Callahan to change her story, too, do you? For God's sake, man, somebody killed her brother. Bradley is one of the men responsible. How can you sit there and lie through your teeth?"

"I'm not lying!"

"The hell you're not!" Slocum took a couple of steps toward the fat man, but threw up his hands in exasperation. He couldn't beat the truth out of Winslow. It wouldn't change anything, even if he did.

"All right, Mr. Winslow, I appreciate your coming by."

"Can I go now?" The fat man looked up, hoping to be dismissed. It was the first sign of life he'd shown since Slocum had arrived.

"Yes," Macomb said, waving a disgusted hand, "you can go."

Winslow got up and crept along the wall, keeping his eyes on Slocum as if he expected to be attacked. It was a reasonable expectation, under the circumstances. He was nearly running by the time he reached the doorway, and he darted through it like a man half his size.

Slocum just stood there, shaking his head.

Macomb stood and hitched up his gun belt. "I never seen the like of it," he said. "The man's scared silly, and he really thinks I believe that garbage."

"No, he doesn't," Slocum said. "But he's too damn scared to care how foolish he looks. Somebody put a real scare into him, and he's looking for any way out."

"If that's true, why didn't they just shoot him? He can't testify if he's dead. Seems like to me a dead man is a lot better than a scared one, if you're interested in keeping something quiet."

"Maybe so, unless he's useful somehow. Maybe he knows them. Maybe he's one of them. Maybe they need him. He's an accountant, right?"

"Supposed to be. What's that got to do with anything?"

"Maybe nothing. Maybe a whole lot. Who's he work for? What was he doing here in the first place?"

Macomb shook his head. "I don't have any idea." He sat back down. "On a different subject, you goin' to the funeral for Callahan this morning?"

Slocum nodded. "Ten thirty."

"You think Miss Callahan would mind if I pay my respects? I didn't know the man, but I got to admit there's something funny here, and somehow I just got to keep scratchin' until I find out what it is. Maybe somebody'll show up at the funeral. Maybe not. But it's a better lead than any I got. Times like this, I wish to Christ I could just haul Bradley out of his cell and whale on his ass until he tells me what he knows."

"You wouldn't be the first sheriff took that approach."

Macomb looked up sharply. His eyes narrowed a bit. "Sounds to me like you're talkin' firsthand. You have a history, Slocum, something I ought to know about?"

"Everybody's got a history, Sheriff. Even you."

Macomb smiled. "Now ain't that the truth?"

"Service is at the cemetery. Miss Callahan didn't want a church service."

"I don't blame her. Preachers make my skin crawl. Don't seem right, somehow, a man lyin' there in a box and some damn fool who never laid eyes on him when he was alive tryin' to tell ever'body how much they gonna miss the corpse. It ain't right."

"I'll see you at the cemetery, Sheriff."

"You can count on it. And, Slocum, if I was you, I'd watch my back. Whatever Winslow's story is, you ain't the same. I know enough about you to know you don't scare easy. That means there's only one way to shut your mouth. They been after Miss Callahan. I got a funny feelin' you might be next. You be careful, boy."

Slocum nodded. "Thanks for the concern."

"Don't go thinkin' I got a soft spot for you. I need a witness I can count on. Winslow's already folded. If Miss

Callahan goes next, you're all I got. I didn't know Will Callahan, but I knew Jake Dalton. And I'm here to tell you, somebody's gonna swing for that old man."

"You'll get no argument from me, Sheriff."

Slocum waved good-bye and headed back to the Royce. Maggie should be just about ready. She wanted to talk to Daniel Parsons a bit before the service, to make sure the mortician understood that she wanted it plain and simple. When Slocum got to her room, he knocked softly, and the door swung open so quickly, he thought she must have been standing with her hand on the knob, already waiting.

She stepped into the hall and closed her door. Wearing a simple black dress with a black hat and veil, she took his hand in both of hers. "You're going to have to help me through this, John. I'll never make it alone."

She let go of his hand and started down the hallway. The lobby was empty, and she paused before stepping out into the heat. Taking a deep breath, she looked up at Slocum and tried to smile. Her heart wasn't in it.

He took her arm and led her outside. The walk to Parsons's Mortuary seemed to take forever. The mortician, an oily scarecrow who smelled of gladiolus and mustache wax, met them at the door. He nodded to Slocum. "Good morning, Miss Callahan," he said.

"Mr. Parsons, I just want to make sure that you understand how serious I am about my instructions."

"Oh, I know. Believe me, Miss Callahan, we are scrupulous indeed in observing our clients' wishes. I already told Reverend Jacobs to keep his remarks brief."

"I told you I didn't want a preacher."

"But I thought you would change your mind, so I took the liberty. It's unchristian, after all."

"Tell him he won't be needed, Mr. Parsons."

"But—"

"Tell him."

Parsons swallowed hard. "Whatever you say, Miss Callahan."

"Then I want to get this over with. Can we go now?"

"I'll see to it, Miss Callahan. Please, just excuse me for a moment." He disappeared into the back. Slocum heard a mumbled conversation. He watched Maggie, who seemed to have regained a little life. Her anger had rekindled her spirit a little. Her eyes looked brighter, as if she were seeing the world around her for the first time that morning.

When Parsons returned, he said, "It's all taken care of, Miss Callahan. If you'll follow me, please."

"We just have to wait for one person," she said. "Mr. Winslow should be here any minute."

"I don't think so, Miss Callahan," Slocum said.

"But I told him I wanted to move the service up. I'm sure he'll—"

"Trust me, Miss Callahan," Slocum said. "He won't be here."

She turned sharply to stare at him, one hand rising toward her mouth. "What's happened? They didn't hurt—"

Slocum stopped her with a raised hand. "No, nothing like that. I'll tell you about it later."

"All right." She seemed confused again, the brightness gone. "Whatever you say." Turning to the mortician, she said, "I guess we can go, then."

Parsons led them through the back and outside, where a hearse was waiting, its black horses pawing the dusty ground and snorting nervously. Behind the hearse was a second wagon, draped in black crepe, with three bench seats arranged across the wagon bed. Black-clad drivers held the reins of both wagons.

Slocum helped Maggie into the wagon while Parsons hovered at his elbow. When she was seated, Slocum climbed in after her. Parsons went to the hearse and climbed up into the seat beside the driver.

The clucks of the drivers and the slap of the reins on the backs of the horses sounded somehow muted. They started out, the creaking of the wheels the only sound. No one spoke in either wagon. The cemetery was a bleak array of small white headstones and weathered wooden markers, if anything, even bleaker than the surrounding desert.

Slocum saw the open grave. The mound of soil, already dry as the dirt around it, seemed poised to slide back into the ground. Slocum shook his head, and Maggie turned to see what he was looking at. When she saw the grave, she reached out and grabbed his forearm with both hands. He felt the fingers digging into his flesh like pincers.

She looked up at him for a moment and let go with one hand. Quickly, she raised the free hand over her hat, caught the black veil in her fingers and lowered it over her face.

"Oh, God, Slocum," she said. "Oh, God, oh, God."

15

Slocum was just leaving Maggie's room when he heard loud voices on the hotel stairs. It sounded as if two men were arguing, but he couldn't tell what about. He stood there with his hand on the knob as the voices grew louder. A moment later, Lieutenant Chamberlain turned the corner, followed by Vance Macomb.

The sheriff spotted Slocum and said, "There he is."

Chamberlain stopped in his tracks and waved a hand. "Slocum, come here," he shouted.

Slocum held his ground.

"You hear me?" Chamberlain shouted. "Come here."

"I expect Mr. Slocum is used to a little more courtesy than you've mustered, Lieutenant," Macomb said. "The polite thing to do is to go to him."

"Shit!" Chamberlain snapped. But he moved. He had his riding gloves in his left hand and started to smack them against his thigh as he walked down the hall. He left no doubt in Slocum's mind what he'd prefer to be hitting with them.

Macomb trailed along behind, shaking his head as if he didn't understand how a man could be so rude.

Chamberlain planted himself in front of Slocum. Without preamble, he said, "You're coming with me, Slocum."

"Why?"

"I need you to show me around the scene of the robbery."

"There's nothing to see, Lieutenant. No reason to make the trip."

"There is if I say there is."

"Sheriff," Slocum said, "do I have to cooperate?"

"No, you don't. But I'd appreciate it if you would. We're all after the same thing. Some of us go about it with a little more patience and some better manners, that's all."

Chamberlain glared at the sheriff, but said nothing. He turned back to Slocum and stood with his legs spread apart, almost as if he expected Slocum to assault him. He tapped the gloves against his thigh, more gently, but no less rapidly. "Well?" he finally asked.

"I don't see what good it'll do."

"Let me decide that, Slocum."

"You coming, Sheriff?"

Macomb shook his head. "Nope. I got business to tend to right here."

"What about Winslow and Miss Callahan? They coming along?"

"Winslow's useless," Macomb said. "And I don't think Miss Callahan's up to it. That leaves you. And it's up to you. You don't want to, it's okay by me."

Slocum thought it over. Letting his breath out in a long, whistling sigh, he refilled his lungs and nodded. "All right, I'll go. But I still think it's a waste of time." Looking at Chamberlain, he said, "But you lean on me too hard and I'm gone. You understand?"

"Don't threaten me, Slocum. I can get a court order forcing you to comply."

"Maybe you ought to do that, then. It'll take a couple of days. In the meantime, there's nothing to stop me from moving on. I'm cooperating voluntarily, and I think you ought to remember that at least, if not appreciate it."

That seemed to make some impression on the lieutenant, and he nodded. "Fair enough."

"All right, then. Meet me at the livery stable in twenty minutes."

Slocum went to his room, left his jacket, and got his Winchester and a box of shells. He grabbed his canteen, draped it over his shoulder, and looped his binocular case on top of it. He was closing his door when he heard Maggie's door open.

She stepped into the hall. When she heard where he was going, she said, "John, I don't like this. I don't like that man, and I don't like the way he's treating you."

Slocum shrugged. "That's what happens when you lose a war," he said.

"No, it's more than that. I can feel it. I wish you weren't going with him."

"I'll be all right."

She stood on tiptoe and leaned forward to peck him on the cheek. "Be careful, please."

He nodded. "Don't worry."

When he got to the end of the hall, he glanced back. She was still standing in the hall, one hand on the doorframe. He waved, but her response was a vague movement of her hand, as if her mind were on something else.

Out in the street, he spotted Chamberlain, already mounted, with two troopers. As he drew close, Chamberlain waved his hand. "Come on, man. Hurry up," he shouted.

Slocum didn't change his pace. He went into the livery stable, mounted his horse, and told the stableman he'd be back later in the day and to keep the space for him. He gave the man two dollars, and swung into the saddle. Nudging the chestnut outside, he found Chamberlain already digging in his spurs. The troopers looked at him with undisguised curiosity. They were just kids, probably recent enlistees. Life out here was still an adventure for them. They looked so much alike, they could have been twin brothers.

They kicked their mounts and fell in behind Slocum, as he moved up on Chamberlain's left. "What are you looking for, exactly?" Slocum asked.

"I don't know. There might be something. I'll know when we get there."

"Lieutenant, I think maybe we ought to declare a truce. At least for the duration."

Chamberlain turned to stare at him. His face was a rigid mask of contorted muscle. "I lost three brothers in the Civil War, Slocum. Maybe you killed one of them. Maybe some brother or cousin of yours killed one of them. Understand?"

"No truce, right?"

"No truce."

"Fine. Just so we know where we stand."

"I do. You figure it out for yourself, Reb."

Slocum nodded. "I already have." Slocum nudged his horse out ahead, and stayed there. For the next four hours, neither man spoke.

It was nearly four o'clock when they drew close to the notch where the stage had been attacked. Slocum reined in and waited for Chamberlain to join him. He pointed toward the shallow mouth of the notch. "That's where it happened," he said. "A couple hundred yards inside, where the walls get higher and more vertical. Three of them were waiting for the stage. The two men on our tail must have been there almost from the time the stage left Yuma."

Chamberlain shielded his eyes with his left hand. "Doesn't look like a bad place for an ambush."

"It wasn't. We buried the proof this morning."

Turning in the saddle, Chamberlain looked back the way they'd come. "Which way did the two men approach from?"

Slocum pointed again. "That way, from the southwest."

"And there were two of them?"

"Yeah."

"When did the driver notice them?"

"Just about here. That's when he whipped the team and pushed on into the notch. I guess he figured they were the problem. Instead, he drove right into it. The stage was handicapped some by the three horses we were trailing. But—"

"Clever plan."

"If you like that sort of thing."

"All right, show me where it happened."

Slocum urged the chestnut forward. Chamberlain stayed right with him this time. It took ten minutes to reach the opening into the ravine. Chamberlain called a halt and dismounted. Slocum joined him on the ground. The two troopers stayed on their mounts and Chamberlain turned on them. "What the hell are you waiting for? Dismount!"

The two young soldiers looked at one another, shrugged, and slipped out of the saddle. Chamberlain grunted in annoyance. "All right, Slocum, show me what happened."

Slocum walked forward, pulling his horse along behind him. Once or twice he knelt to get a closer look at the ground. The wheel marks of the stage were still visible. The wind had sifted dirt into the ruts, but not enough to fill them completely.

Checking his memory against the terrain, he found the spot where the stage had stopped. Off to the right, he rubbed the ground with the flat of his hand. "Should be right here somewhere," he said.

"What are you looking for?" Chamberlain demanded.

"You'll know when I find it."

Hunching forward a few inches, he dropped to all fours, using his right hand to scrape away the accumulated soil. Glancing once more at the walls towering above him, he moved again, then bent close to the ground and blew away the dirt.

A few seconds later, the dark stain of Will Callahan's blood materialized. "All right," Slocum said, pointing at the bloodstain, "this is where Callahan lay when they shot him."

He pointed to the left. "That's where the stage was. The three men in ambush came out of those rocks off to the right. I didn't see them at first, but it's the only logical place."

Looking up at Chamberlain, who had moved a few feet closer, he said, "I still don't see what you hope to gain from all this."

Chamberlain waved the objection away. "Don't worry about it."

The two troopers were standing just behind Slocum. One of them dropped to one knee. He leaned forward and Slocum shifted his body to the right to let the kid get a closer look.

He heard a loud thump, as if a ripe apple had fallen from a tree. He was turning his head toward the sound when he heard the crack. Instantly, he knew what had happened. "Get down," he shouted.

Ducking to his right, he scrambled for the rocks, trying to get out of the line of fire. He heard Chamberlain shout something and turned to see the second trooper racing toward him.

The soldier who had been kneeling beside him lay on the sand. He wasn't moving. The stain of Will Callahan's blood was obscured by new blood seeping into the sand. Slocum saw the ugly hole on the side of the trooper's head and turned away.

A second rifle shot cracked from somewhere high above him, toward the top of the wall, maybe even over it. The slug chipped the rocks to Slocum's left, then whined off and slammed into the ground.

Chamberlain and the other trooper were on the opposite side of the notch. Chamberlain waved a hand. "You all right over there, Slocum?"

"Yeah," he shouted. There was no sign of the gunman. Using his binoculars to trace the rimrock, he scanned from directly above him to a place nearly two hundred yards ahead, where the the edge had fallen away, leaving a gap of several yards in the otherwise straight edge.

"Apaches," Chamberlain shouted.

"I don't think so," Slocum answered.

Chamberlain pointed his Colt Army at the rim and fired three times. Chunks of rock split off from the lip of the ravine and showered down onto the boulders below. The fire was not returned.

"They're gone, looks like," Chamberlain shouted.

Who's gone? Slocum wondered. He glanced back at the unmoving body of the young soldier. He replayed in his mind the last few seconds before the first shot had been fired. And every time, he came to the same conclusion. The shot had been meant for him. If the kid hadn't wanted to get a better look at the bloodstain, Slocum would have taken the slug.

And an interesting question occurred to him. Just how much did Lieutenant Walter Chamberlain really know about this?

16

Slocum swung into his saddle. He knew Chamberlain was watching him, and he didn't give a damn.

"Where the hell you going, Slocum?" the lieutenant demanded.

"I'm through answering to you, Chamberlain. You got a man killed for nothing. If you think I'm going to wait around until it's my turn, you're crazy."

"You rebs are all the same. Yellow. No wonder we whipped your ass. You don't have the guts to stand your ground."

Slocum eased the chestnut toward Chamberlain. He walked the animal slowly, said nothing. When he was abreast of the lieutenant, he leaned over in the saddle until he was staring directly into Chamberlain's face. "You want to say that again, Lieutenant?"

Chamberlain turned away.

"I didn't think so," Slocum said. He dug in his spurs and pushed the chestnut into a gallop. Chamberlain suddenly recovered his voice and shouted something after him. Slocum didn't catch the words, and he didn't give a damn.

He pushed the stallion hard all the way back to Yuma. It was after dark by the time he reached the town limits.

Pulling up in front of Macomb's office, he jumped from the saddle, letting the reins drag in the dust.

The office door was closed and bolted. Rapping hard on the door, he leaned over to peer through the dusty window. Brady Anderson was sitting behind the desk, a loaded shotgun leaning against the wall right beside him. He saw Slocum and moved to the door.

Slocum heard the bolt being drawn, and the clunk of the heavy bar on the floor when Anderson jerked it free. The door swung back, and Anderson, a pistol in his hand, stood in the doorway. "Slocum, what do you want?"

"Sheriff around?"

"He's over to home, I guess. Why?"

"We got to talk."

"He lives in the Yuma Hotel, right across the street. Want me to go get him?"

"No, Brady, you stay right here. I'll wait till you lock up."

The second guard on duty shouted to Anderson from inside the cellblock, asking if anything was wrong. Brady reassured him, then stepped back inside and closed the door. When the bar thudded home, Slocum crossed the street and entered the lobby of the Yuma Hotel.

The night clerk was reading a newspaper, and Slocum had to pound on the bell before he could get the clerk's attention.

In that supercilious tone mastered by clerks of every kind, he asked, "May I help you?"

"Sheriff Macomb in?"

"Upstairs. Room 2D." He was back to his newspaper before Slocum could have asked a second question. Rapping his knuckles on the desk until he reached its end, Slocum jogged to the stairs, took them two at a time, and walked briskly down the hall. He found 2D with no trouble, and rapped on the door.

"Who is it?" Macomb called from somewhere inside.

"It's me, Slocum."

"Hold your water." Footsteps approached the door, and

when it swung open, Macomb stood there in his jeans and long-john shirt. His feet were bare and a fat cigar jutted out of his mouth at a steep angle. "What's the problem now, Slocum? Jesus, I'm getting sick of lookin' at your ugly face."

"What do you know about Walter Chamberlain?"

"What's to know? He's a tight-assed lieutenant like all tight-assed lieutenants. Kind of guy you love to hate. Why?"

"Because he got one of his men killed this afternoon. Only I think it was an accident."

"Now hold on. You can't have it both ways, Slocum. Either he got a man killed or it was an accident, in which case he didn't do anything. It just happened."

"I think it was supposed to be me."

"What?"

"The kid who got killed was kneeling right beside me. I moved just as the shooter cut loose. The kid doesn't move, I don't move either, and then it'd be me who stops the bullet."

"What'd Chamberlain say?"

"Said it was Apaches."

"You see any redskins?"

"None."

"I see. How come he brung you all the way out there, anyhow? I didn't understand what good it would do, but I thought I ought to go along. Sometimes I need the army, so I can't exactly tell them to go jump when they need something from me. In this case, that meant you."

"Can I come in?"

"Jesus," Macomb said. "I'm sorry. I forgot my manners. Come on in." He stepped away from the door, waited for Slocum to enter, then pushed it closed.

There was only one chair in the room, so Macomb sat on the bed. He waved a hand to take in the meager furnishings. "It ain't much, is it?"

Slocum smiled. "Beats a hole in the ground."

"But not by much. I used to live in a house, like a normal

17

"Where you going?" Macomb asked.

"Miss Callahan is in danger. I'm going to make sure she's all right."

"You really don't think our accountant killed himself, do you?"

"No, I don't, Sheriff. And I don't think you believe it, either. They already killed Cartwright, they tried to kill me, and now they've killed Winslow. And they tried to get into Miss Callahan's room at the hotel. That tells me two things."

"Which are?"

"It tells me that they won't stop at killing a woman. And it tells me that this is a lot more than a simple holdup. There has got to be something much bigger here. Nobody goes to all this trouble for something like that."

"Too damn bad all that don't tell you who *they* might be, Slocum. Or does it?"

"Not yet, but it will. In the meantime, you better make sure Bradley is protected, too. Now that they know they can't bust him out, they likely will decide to kill him, too."

"I was thinking the same thing. You better keep an eye on the Callahan woman tonight, and tomorrow we'll make arrangements for her. In the meantime, I think I'll spend the night at the office, after I tend to this business. I want to take a look around here, see can I turn up something that explains any of this." Macomb knelt beside the body of Ralph Winslow again. "Poor bastard," he said. He reached out to close the staring eyes with his thumb.

Slocum ran to the Royce and pounded up the stairs. He was out of breath when he reached Maggie's door. Pausing a moment to regain it, he knocked softly. "Miss Callahan," he called, trying to keep his voice under control. "You there?"

He knocked again. It seemed like an eternity before he heard a noise from beyond the door. Another until the knob turned and the door swung back.

"What's wrong, John? What's happened?"

"Ralph Winslow is dead."

She buried her face in her hands. "My God! They're going to kill us all, aren't they?"

Slocum stepped through the doorway, gently pushing Maggie aside with his hands on her shoulders, then closed the door and locked it. To be on the safe side, he jammed a ladder-back chair under the knob. Pulling her hands away from her face, he said, "Miss Callahan, listen to me. I have to stay here tonight. You're not safe here by yourself."

She nodded, but her eyes were glazed and he wasn't certain she understood. He went to the window and pulled it down, then locked it. Slocum tugged the drapes closed, then looked around the room for something more substantial to cover the window. The only thing available was a chest of drawers which came halfway up, but it would have to do. He wrestled the furniture across the floor until it blocked the lower half. A least a random shot through the window wouldn't hit them.

When he was satisfied, he turned to see Maggie still standing by the door, her shoulders hunched and her arms hugged across her stomach as if she were cold. "I'm frightened, John. I don't understand what's happening, and I'm frightened."

He nodded. "It'll be all right, Miss Callahan. Tomorrow we'll move you to someplace where you can be protected."

"No, you don't understand what I mean. I'm not afraid someone will hurt me or even kill me. It's not knowing why all this is happening that I find so frightening. I mean, my brother is dead, and I don't know why. That old man is dead, and that boy, too. And now Ralph. Why?"

"If we knew that, maybe we could put a stop to it. I think Winslow knew something. I think that's why they didn't kill him earlier. But they spooked for some reason. Why was he here? Do you know? You mentioned an audit, but what kind? Who for?"

She shrugged. "He talked a lot, you know that. You saw him in action. But I didn't pay that much attention to him. He was just a noise in the background most of the time, like the wind or the rain. You know it's there, but you don't actually pay attention. At least I didn't."

"But you must remember something. You know he was an accountant. What was he doing in Yuma?"

"I don't know, that audit or something, but I don't know any more than that. He talked about it, I suppose, but—"

"Audit of what? Think, Miss Callahan, please."

"John, I think you can call me Maggie, don't you? After all, we've been—well, you know what I mean."

He was startled by the abrupt change of subject, but shook his head. "All right then, Maggie. What was he auditing? Did he work for the government? Some company? What?"

"I don't know. The government, I think. I mean, he told us all about these politicians he knew back East so— I'm just not sure."

"You have to think."

"I can't think now. I'm too frightened. Let me sleep on it. Maybe I'll remember something, but it's hard to know what you're looking for. I just—" She shook her head in exasperation.

She looked so vulnerable and so small. Barefoot, she lost a couple of inches. She was still tall, nearly five eight,

Slocum guessed, but her height was not so imposing now. "I'm so tired," she said. "I have to sleep."

"You go ahead."

Maggie walked to the bed and stopped at the night table long enough to turn the lamp low. She sat on the bed and pulled a sheet over her legs. She shucked off her shirt and tossed it onto the floor. Under the sheet, she removed her jeans, dumped them on top of the shirt, then lay back and pulled the sheet up under her chin.

"Aren't you coming to bed?" she asked.

"No, I don't think so." He bent to pull off his boots and set them beside the chair.

"John, you can't sit up all night watching me sleep. It's not that interesting. Besides, if anyone tries to get in here, we'll know. It would take a battering ram to knock down the door, and the window is secure."

He shook his head. "No, I don't think so."

She moved closer to the far edge of the bed. Patting the mattress, she said, "There's plenty of room, see? Right here."

When he didn't respond, she said, "Good night, John. I'm sure I won't be able to sleep, so if I think of anything, I'll let you know."

"Good night, Miss Calla—Maggie."

"That's better," she said.

He walked to the night table and turned out the lamp. He found the single chair without much difficulty and sat. He looked at the window. With the drapes drawn so tightly, the room was pitch black. He couldn't even see the outline of the window frame beyond the drapes. The moon would be up later, but for the moment he might as well have been in a coffin.

The air in the room was close, and having the window closed was going to make it stifling before long. Sitting there in the dark, he tried to remember the conversation he'd only half heard in the stagecoach, but there was little that had stayed with him. Most of the talk he could recall had been about ranching, Winslow using his accounting knowledge to pontificate on every aspect of the business, Will Callahan, mostly out of politeness, agreeing and asking an occasional question.

He explored the entire conversation twice, and came up empty. There had been nothing, at least nothing he'd overheard or that had been addressed to him, to suggest what Winslow had been working on, why he was in Yuma, or who he worked for. The man was a blowhard, and Slocum found it difficult to believe that a man could talk so much and say so little.

The light had been out for more than an hour. Maggie hadn't spoken, but he knew she wasn't asleep. Her movements were too controlled, as if she were trying not to make noise. He could hear the hiss of the sheet on her skin as she turned one way or another and once, he thought, she had turned over.

He jumped when something thumped near the bed; then he realized she had plumped her pillow, raised it, and slapped it back against the mattress.

The sheet hissed again. He knew, without being able to see her clearly, that Maggie was sitting up.

"I can't sleep," she said, her voice plaintive, that of a small child the night before school opened.

"You're not trying." He laughed, remembering how many times he'd heard those same words from his parents.

"What's so funny?"

He didn't answer. He heard the sheet again. It was hard to avoid imagining the contours of her body, the smoothness of her skin, the play of supple muscles along her back and thighs. But he tried.

He heard a violent motion on the bed, as if she had turned her back to him and pulled the sheet up over her head. He was curious, but didn't want to ask. He let the minutes tick away, and for a long time there was no further sound.

Her breathing was still restrained, so he knew she wasn't sleeping. He was tired, and he closed his eyes. He knew Maggie was right; any attempt to break in would wake him in plenty of time. He found himself drifting off to sleep and decided not to fight it. It was enough that he was here.

Something brushed against his cheek and he turned his head, but it persisted. He reached up, thinking to chase an insect away, only to brush the back of his hand against something cool. He came awake slowly, dimly aware of someone standing over him.

He reached up again as his cheek was tickled once more. This time he knew it was a lock of hair. He tangled it in his fingers, pulling her toward him. He felt her lips on his forehead, then they traced his hairline and brushed his ear. "I can't sleep, John. You have to do something." The throaty whisper sent chills up his spine.

"What do you have in mind?"

"Think of something," she said. She lowered herself onto his lap and bent to kiss him. He let one hand slide along her rib cage until it found a breast. He closed his hand over it, feeling the nub of the nipple against his palm. It pushed back against his skin as he squeezed gently, then found the nipple with his thumb. Circling the thumb, he felt the nipple harden, the aureole pebble and grow hot.

Bending his head, he sucked the nipple into his mouth, letting his tongue swirl against it. He sucked harder, filling his mouth with the firm flesh. She twitched then, pulling her breast away, then turned to bring the other close. He felt it brush his chin, and sought it eagerly. The nipple was already hard, and he twirled his tongue over the smooth skin.

His free hand was in her lap, and he played with the curls, tracing the outline of her bush then sliding the hand along one solid thigh and back again. Her legs parted as she shifted her weight, and he went lower now, feeling the glazed lips with his fingertips.

She moaned in his ear. "Nice," she whispered. "So nice." He played with the auburn thatch, letting his fingers slide through the curls, then between the thickening lips. She switched her hips every time his fingers drew close, and he finally took the hint, letting one slide into the warm slickness of her. She moved her hips to take the finger in deeper. His thumb found the nub of her, and he circled it, feeling the hardness of it. He moved his hand now, withdrawing the finger, but she moved her hips again to keep it there.

"More," she whispered.

He slid the finger in and out. Her breathing grew raspy as he increased the tempo, short sharp breaths hissing in his ear as her tongue swirled around, darting in and out.

She started to moan again, then he felt her hips rise and she lifted herself off him and he let the finger slide all the way out. She bent over him them, the tangled mass of her hair tickling his cheeks and then his chest as she worked at his buttons.

Grabbing him by one arm, she pulled him to his feet, undid his belt, and pulled his dungarees down. He stepped out of them and she pulled him toward the bed, then dragged him down onto it.

Her fingers closed over his erection as she lay back. The hiss of her skin on the sheet told him she had spread her legs wide. She pulled him closer, and he planted one knee on the edge of the bed. For a moment he felt the tickle of her bush on the tip of him and then the heat of the parting lips as he slid all the way in.

Her hips were already moving and he caught her rhythm easily this time. He felt her arms encircle him and pull him down. He wished morning would never come.

18

Slocum thought he was in an oven when he woke up. The still air in the room was claustrophobic. He opened his eyes to see Maggie sitting on the bed watching him. She wore an open shirt but no pants, and her legs were tucked under her.

"I've been thinking," she said. "I don't know if it means anything or not, but he told Will he worked for a company in Denver that had a contract with the army."

"Did he say what for?"

"Something about surveying contracts and books. I don't know for sure, because I was trying not to pay attention."

She tossed her head to rearrange her long curls. Her breasts bobbed seductively, but her mind was not on seduction. Neither was Slocum's.

She screwed up her face, trying to concentrate. "I wish I could remember more, but—you know what he was like. It was so hard to listen to him for very long."

"Do you remember the name of the company?"

"No. I'm sure he said, but I just don't remember. All I remember is that it was in Denver. I suppose that's not much help, is it?"

"Maybe. We'll have to see."

"What do we do now?"

"Macomb is going to make arrangements for you to go someplace safe. Maybe he already has."

She seemed alarmed at the prospect. "Go where?"

"I don't know, Maggie. But it has to be done. You're in danger here."

"I don't want to be separated from you, John, not now, not when we're just getting to know one another."

Slocum smiled. He reached out for her, pulled her down on top of him, and slid one hand under the back of her shirt. He let his fingers rest on her shoulder blades. With the other hand, he brushed the hair away from her face. "I don't want anything to happen to you, Maggie."

"But—"

He put a finger across her lips. "Shsssh—there's nothing to talk about. You have to do it. It won't be for long."

She wriggled off him and sat again, pulling the shirt tight across her chest, as if she were suddenly cold. Gnawing on her lower lip, she watched him. "You don't seem upset about it."

"Should I be?"

She shrugged. "I would hope so."

"Maggie, I'm not like you. I've been alone for a long, long time. I've gotten used to it."

"Does that mean you can't get unused to it?"

"No."

"Then try. Would you, please?"

He smiled. Pulling her down again, he kissed the top of her head. When she straightened, he patted her rump. "You'd better get dressed. We should get to Macomb's office soon. And make sure you pack everything you'll need."

She crawled off the bed, and he got up. He moved the chest of drawers away from the window, pulled the drapes aside. Unlocking the sash, he raised it until it thumped against the top of the frame. Staring out into the heat, he watched the desert for a long time.

"What are you thinking?" Maggie asked.

"Nothing."

"Yes, you are."

He turned then, still holding the drapes aside. She stood there naked, a fresh shirt dangling from one hand. Even the harsh sunlight couldn't erase the easy curve of her hips, the long line of her legs. Her breasts, if anything, looked fuller, firmer, than under the soft glow of the lamp.

"You're a beautiful woman," he said.

"You're not going to tell me, are you? What you were thinking, I mean."

"It doesn't matter."

"Have it your way." She jammed one arm into a sleeve, and for the next ten minutes the only sounds in the room were those of flesh and cloth in angry contact.

When they were both dressed, Slocum buckled on his gun belt and picked up her carpetbag. "You have everything you want to take with you?"

"Almost," she said, sticking her tongue out at him.

"Let's go, then."

Macomb was waiting in his office when they got there. "Miss Callahan," he said, "we got to get you out of town for your own protection."

She looked at Slocum, but didn't argue with the sheriff. "Mr. Slocum told me."

"I know it's an inconvenience, but I think it's best. You're pretty fair on a horse, I understand, so it'd be best if we went that way, just the three of us. I got some people who'll take care of you. First, I was thinking to run you over to Fort Hillman, but it's too damn far. My brother was in town yesterday, and I got to thinkin' maybe his place was the best bet, so we worked it out. Besides, I think Mr. Slocum has some suspicions about the army, and I'm starting to think he's right."

"Why's that, Sheriff?"

"We'll talk about it on the way. Then I think we'll go on to Hillman ourselves."

Slocum was curious, but he thought it best not to push

Macomb, at least not in front of Maggie. The less she had to worry about, the better off she'd be.

Macomb said, "I took the liberty of gettin' your mounts ready. They're out behind the jail. We might as well get going." He turned to two men who were seated on the floor in the corner. "You boys know what to do. You got any problems, you talk to Brady. He's in charge till I get back, probably tomorrow."

"Don't worry about it, Vance," the larger of the two said. "We can handle it."

"See that you do, Roy. I get back and find Bradley gone, I'll skin you both."

Roy slapped his thigh and laughed. "Need a sharp knife on this old hide, Vance."

Macomb led them out the door and through the alley to the back. The horses shifted nervously until Slocum took his chestnut's reins and stroked its muzzle. He waited for Maggie to mount up, then swung into his own saddle.

"Where we headed, Sheriff?" Slocum asked.

"Charlie, that's my brother, lives over near the Gila River. He's got a big spread and three of the strappingest boys you'd ever want to see. Miss Callahan'll be fine there. Charlie and the boys'll see to that. Mabel's a good woman, that's Charlie's wife, Miss Callahan. Reads too much for my taste, but I expect you two'll get along just fine."

"I was beginning to think there were no books west of the Mississippi, Sheriff," she said. "It'll be a nice change to sit down with one."

"If she lets you. She'll probably talk your ear off. Charlie don't read at all, and the boys got better things to do, so I reckon she don't have no one to talk to about whatever she does read."

He kicked his mount and led the way out of town. As they left Yuma behind, Slocum glanced back, concerned that they not be followed. He knew Macomb was right, but he didn't like the idea of leaving Maggie. He didn't want her to know that, so he said nothing.

The ride to Charlie Macomb's took the better part of two hours. But it was worth it, Slocum thought. On the banks of the Gila River, the spread was an island of rich green nestled in a bowllike valley. The river wandered aimlessly, wide and shallow. On either side of the broad valley, the mountains seemed to spring out of the ground at a steep angle and there was nothing but rocky wasteland as far as the eye could see.

The terrain of Arizona amazed Slocum. Raised in the lush Eastern forests and rich farmlands, he'd found the adjustment to the sea of grass enough of a stretch. But the barrenness of the Southwestern desert was almost farther than his mind could reach. And the suddenness with which rich green could spring up along the edges of the few sources of water was almost miraculous. He had seen valleys full of thick vegetation, stood on bare rock ledges with nothing but dust and dry yellow behind him, and looked down at them almost as if they were mirages.

Charlie Macomb met them at the end of the winding lane that led to his house. He had a shotgun draped over one arm and a pistol stuck in his belt. He nodded to his brother, glanced at Slocum, and gave Maggie a huge smile. "My God, Vance," he said, "she's even better lookin' than you said. And she's a good-sized gal, too, ain't she?" He grinned at the sheriff, who turned beet red and told his brother to shut up.

Slocum was laughing so hard that Maggie took a swipe at him.

"May as well come on down and get something to eat," Charlie said. "You folks must be hungry and thirsty."

"No time, Charlie, thanks all the same. If you just take Miss Callahan down to Mabel, me and Slocum'll be on our way."

"You sure, Vance?"

The sheriff nodded. "Unless Slocum wants to set a spell." He glanced over, but Slocum shook his head no.

"All right, then." He reached over to grab Slocum's hand. "Pleased to meet you. And don't let this big bear maul you to death, Slocum. Vance is all gums and no teeth, no matter the growling he likes to do."

"I already figured that out, Charlie," Slocum said.

Charlie Macomb turned his horse. "Come on, then, Miss Callahan, you just follow me. You be careful, Vance," he shouted over his shoulder as his big bay broke into a trot. "You, too, Slocum."

Maggie followed the big man, but she kept glancing back over her shoulder, as if to make certain that Slocum was still there.

"That gal's kind of sweet on you, son," Macomb said. "Nice catch, she is, too."

"Too good for me, Sheriff."

"Never met a woman yet who wasn't too good for any man. That's the way God planned it, I reckon."

Anxious to change the subject, Slocum asked, "What did you want to tell me about?" He kept his eyes on Maggie and waved when she headed through a stand of cottonwoods and out of sight for a while. When she reached the other side of the trees, he could no longer see her face clearly, and finally looked at Macomb.

"Well, I don't rightly know for sure what it means. But Winslow had a mess of papers with him in a case under his bed. Made me wonder whether whoever killed him, if it wasn't suicide—and I got to admit you're probably right about that—was lookin' for them."

"What kind of papers?"

"Everything from reports to accounts. There was a part of a ledger there, and a bunch of letters. Mostly to or from some outfit called Dale and Mitchell, up in Denver. Must be the fellas he worked for, I figure."

"They tell you anything?"

"What, the papers? Hell no. I don't know nothing about accounting. Years back, I run a store for a few years. Had all I could do to keep track of my inventory and accounts. Finally went bust, and I swear it was because of them numbers. Never did get the hang of it."

"Be interesting to talk to the commanding officer at

Hillman about them, though, wouldn't it?"

"If they have something to do with the payroll, sure would." He reached back and slapped his saddlebags. "That's why I brung 'em along."

19

Colonel Stanley Martin was the tallest man Slocum had ever seen. Standing six feet six inches tall in his stocking feet, the heels of his boots gave him the appearance of another two to three inches. He looked almost slight, until you looked closely. The hand he extended to Slocum seemed to be the size of a dinner plate, and there was nothing frail about the grip.

His sun-darkened skin resembled the cover of the Slocum family Bible in color and in toughness. The colonel nodded in time to the handshake, then reached out to clap Macomb on the shoulder.

"Vance," he said, "what can I do for you?"

Macomb rubbed his right thigh with an open palm. "I'm not sure, Stan. I'm really not sure."

"Well, hell, Vance, you didn't ride all the way out here for nothing, that much I know. We go back a few years, so you can level with me. What's on your mind?"

"You have a lieutenant here, a man named Walter Chamberlain. Is that right?"

Martin lowered himself into the huge chair behind his desk. "That's right, I do. Sent him over to talk to you a couple days ago."

"I met him, yes."

"He give you a problem?"

Macomb looked at Slocum. "Maybe you better take it from here," he said.

Martin leaned forward, propping himself up on the desk top with splayed elbows.

"How long has Chamberlain been assigned here, Colonel?"

"A year, more or less. Probably a little more. I can check for you, if you want the exact date."

"Before the first payroll robbery?"

"That's a strange question, Mr. Slocum. You have any particular reason for asking it?"

"Maybe."

"As a matter of fact, Lieutenant Chamberlain got here about two months before the first robbery. Are you suggesting there's a connection?"

"No. Why? Do you think there might be one?"

"No reason to think that. And I don't mind telling you, Mr. Slocum, I'm not certain I like where you're going with this."

"I'm not sure I know where I'm going, Colonel. But I don't think there's any reason to avoid pursuing the question. It's not an accusation, after all, just a question."

"You have some reason to dislike Lieutenant Chamberlain, Mr. Slocum?"

"He almost got me killed, Colonel."

"He told me about that. Said you were jumped by Apaches. And that young trooper we lost, McLoughlin, was a fine young man. You were lucky, as I understand it."

"I'd agree with that, Colonel, but not the way you mean it. There were no Apaches."

"How much do you know about Apaches, Mr. Slocum?"

"Enough."

"Did you see the man who shot McLoughlin?"

"Not clearly, no. But he was no Apache. That shot was meant for me. There's no doubt in my mind about that."

"Tell me something, Mr. Slocum. If Chamberlain was so

interested in burying you, why didn't he just shoot you in the back and leave you out there in the desert?"

"Because there were witnesses, Colonel. Two of them."

"All right, let's say I accept that. What reason would he have?"

"If I'm right, if he has something to do with one or more of your payroll robberies, he has all the reason he needs. Two witnesses have already been killed. A third has been attacked. There's a pattern there, it looks like to me. And I think Lieutenant Chamberlain figures in it somewhere, but I don't know exactly where."

"That's a mighty serious charge to level at any man, Mr. Slocum."

"I understand that, Colonel. And I want you to be perfectly clear on what I'm saying. I think there's something rotten here, and right now there's no better candidate than Lieutenant Chamberlain. I could be wrong. But what if I'm right? What then? Don't you think it's important enough at least to consider the possibility?"

Martin ran a hand through his long white hair. He fussed with a stray lock that wouldn't stay put, twisted it into a tight curl, then let go. "All right," he said, "go ahead."

"Did a man named Ralph Winslow have any connection with this post?"

Martin snorted. "That windbag? He was here, yes. He audited the books. When he could shut up long enough to do it, that is."

"And what was the result of that audit?"

"I don't know. I haven't seen the report yet. As far as I know, it's not finished."

"Then it's not going to be finished, Colonel."

"Why in hell not? Winslow's company is under contract. He has to finish it. That's what they're getting paid for."

"Winslow's dead, Colonel."

"What?"

"He was one of the witnesses we mentioned. Somebody stabbed him to death and made a lousy attempt at making it look like he killed himself."

"Stan," Macomb said, "what was he working on? Was there some special reason he was here, or was it just a normal thing?"

"I'm not really at liberty to disclose that, Vance. I'm sorry."

"Stan, come on, like you said, we go back a ways. I got people droppin' like flies in Yuma, and Slocum thinks your boy Chamberlain is right smack in the middle of it. Now, I got a right to know whether he's on the mark or way off base. I can't know that unless you tell me whatever you know."

Martin shook his head. "I'd like to help, Vance, but I can't."

"Can't or won't?" Slocum snapped.

Macomb reached out with one hand as if to snatch the words out of the air before Martin heard them. "Slocum, you shouldn't be—"

"Let it go, Vance," Martin said. "If I were in Mr. Slocum's shoes, I guess I'd be pretty damn mad, too. He's got a right. But I have my orders, and I can't ignore them."

"Colonel," Slocum said, "we're talking about lives here. This is not just a matter of saving your ass or your career. We're talking about people dying, innocent people."

"Soldiers are no less innocent, Mr. Slocum. And when they die, they bleed just like civilians. They get the same pine box and they have the same damn granite for their headstones. Don't lecture me about the sanctity of human life. I've spent my whole life doing my damnedest to protect it. That may sound odd coming from a military man, but a good soldier keeps people from getting killed unnecessarily. And, Mr. Slocum, I'm one damned good soldier."

Slocum leaned back in his chair. "All right, Colonel, forget about the audit. Suppose you take a look a some papers and tell us if you ever saw any of them before, or if they mean anything to you. Maybe they have something to do with Winslow's death, and maybe they don't."

Martin sighed. "Let me see them."

Macomb jerked his saddlebags off the floor and opened

the right pouch. He plunged one giant hand inside and withdrew a sheaf of papers. He leaned forward to slap them onto Martin's desk.

The colonel pulled the stack of white sheets toward him. He lifted the top sheet, then reached into a desk drawer for a pair of spectacles, hooked the wire frames around his ears, and tugged them into place. Adjusting their perch on his nose, he examined the first paper.

"This is just a letter from Winslow to his office." Looking through the next few, he pushed them aside. "More of the same," he muttered.

The next sheet was different. Slocum could see the cramped columns of figures even from where he sat. It appeared as if Winslow were less expansive on paper than he was in conversation. The tiny figures were not readable from where Slocum sat.

Martin started to speak, then snapped his jaw shut. He put the paper aside, but kept it separate from the others. He looked at Macomb over the top of his spectacles, but said nothing.

"That mean something to you, Stan?" Macomb asked.

"It might. How long are you going to be at Fort Hillman? You staying overnight, or you going back today?"

"Just overnight."

"You mind if I hang onto these until tomorrow? Give me a chance to study them."

"Sure, Stan," Macomb said.

But Slocum wasn't satisfied. "On one condition," he said.

"And what condition is that, Mr. Slocum?" the colonel asked.

"That you don't show them to Chamberlain or tell anybody you have them."

"I don't see—"

"Yes or no, Colonel?" Slocum snapped.

"All right."

"I have another question, Colonel."

Martin was clearly exasperated. "One more, Mr. Slocum.

I have other matters to attend to."

Slocum nodded. "If you didn't see Winslow's report, who did?"

"I don't know that he wrote one."

"Assume he did."

"I'm sure I don't know. It would have gone through channels, of course, and therefore would have been seen by one of the administrative officers, most likely our supply officer."

"And who would that be?"

Martin paused for a moment. Before he answered he narrowed his eyes slightly, as if he were squinting at something he couldn't see quite clearly enough to identify. "Lieutenant Chamberlain," he said.

20

Slocum and the sheriff ate supper at the Martin quarters, a large house at one corner of the oblong compound that was Fort Hillman. The colonel didn't talk much during the meal and when it was finished, he asked them to accompany him to the porch. Once outside, away from his wife and the maid, he opened up a little.

Lowering himself into a swing, he fished a cigar out of his tunic pocket and struck a match on the arm of the swing. Macomb sat in a white rocking chair and Slocum sat on the floor, his back against one of four white columns supporting the porch roof.

Puffing vigorously, Martin finally got the cigar securely lit. He tried for a smoke ring, failed, and tried again. This time, a tight ring of bluish smoke wobbled toward the porch roof, slowly falling apart and finally dissolving to a blur.

Only then did he speak. "How long we known each other, Vance?"

"Five, maybe six years, I guess, Stan. Why?"

"No reason. Just touching base with history, I guess. You wear a uniform as long as I have, and one year looks like another. When you're in a war, everything goes by so fast, you don't notice time passing. When you're not in a war, everything goes by so slowly you lose track. It amounts to the same thing, I guess."

"Something on your mind, Stan? I mean something a calendar couldn't cure?"

"You always were a blunt son of a bitch, Vance." Martin laughed. "No doubt about that."

Macomb tilted his head to one side. "In my line of work," he said, pushing the rocker into motion with one thrust, "you got to come to the point in a hurry. Most times, you don't get to say anythin' at all. Subtlety is wasted air."

Martin puffed his cigar. "What line of work you in, Slocum?" The words were accompanied by puffs of blue smoke.

"Whatever comes along, Colonel."

"How'd you get messed up in this thing?"

"Just lucky, I guess."

"Slocum was on the stage when it was knocked over, Stan. He saw the robbers, and he's one of two witnesses I got left, out of six. Hadn't been for him, I wouldn't have one left."

Martin was quiet for nearly a minute. He leaned forward to knock a clump of ash from the cigar, took another puff, then scratched behind his ear with a fingertip. "I wish I could tell you I resent what you're suggesting, Slocum."

"Colonel, I—"

Martin held up a hand. "Hold on, let me finish. I said I *wish* I could resent it, but the fact of the matter is, I can't. It's not the first time somebody's suggested Walter Chamberlain is out of plumb a little. The thing is, I don't know whether it's true, and if it is, I don't know just how crooked he might be. The problem with my situation is this: Chamberlain is a hardworking officer. He's intelligent, and he's disciplined. But he's also something of a bully. He pushes men, pushes them hard; I think too hard, sometimes. But I can't start undercutting him, or he'd lose his ability to command the men. So, he makes enemies. Since he's— among other things—our supply officer, he makes civilian enemies, too."

"I don't see what you're driving at, Colonel," Slocum said.

"If you make enemies, and your enemies tell somebody something about you, accuse you of something, maybe they're right. But just maybe they're trying to get even with you. People who want to get even aren't particularly constrained by the truth. You see what I mean?"

"I don't see what that has to do with the current situation," Slocum insisted.

"Maybe nothing, Slocum. But if I disregard those accusations against Lieutenant Chamberlain that come from sources that are suspect, or at least less than disinterested, then what you suggest is the first and only accusation of any wrongdoing on his part. I can't hang a man for that."

"So you won't do anything. Is that what you're saying, Colonel?"

"Not exactly. I can't really do anything without reason, evidence, Mr. Slocum. Do you have any? Any that would stand up in a court, that is?"

"No. Not the kind you want."

"Then my hands are almost tied. But not quite. I can watch Chamberlain. I can monitor his activities more closely. But I can't accuse him, and I can't have others aware of your accusations, because it will undermine the order and discipline of this post. This is a backwater." He swept his hands to take in the compound. "You can see that with your own eyes. This is no place to enhance your career. The men who are assigned to this facility are dedicated, or so I want to believe. But I will do what I can to see whether there is any basis for suspicion. Other than that—"

"And if we get you evidence?"

"Obviously, that changes things significantly."

Slocum sucked on his lower lip. He didn't know whether to accept Martin's position at face value, or to look deeper. In the end, it wouldn't much matter. Martin held all the cards.

"You got any other problems here, Stan?" Macomb asked.

"Like?"

"I don't know, missing supplies, Indian troubles, whatever—"

"Supplies, yes. There's a history of that here."

"And you say Chamberlain is your supply officer?" Slocum felt like he'd just been handed an opening.

"Yes, he is. But I already told you, I can't go into that. I—aw, what the hell." He waved a hand in capitulation.

"What's he done about it?"

Martin shrugged. "What he can, I suppose. It's a difficult problem. Shortages are part of the army, as you can well imagine."

"And payroll robbery? Is that part of the army, Colonel?"

Martin bristled. "Of course not."

"But you've had four in the last year. Is there a connection?"

"Not that I know of, no. And I don't think I see what you're driving at, Mr. Slocum."

"Just exploring, Colonel. That's all."

"Of course." Martin took a couple of puffs on the cigar, then tossed it off the porch. He got out of the swing and walked down the steps, where he ground the butt under his heel. With his back to the porch, he surveyed the desolate outpost. "You're welcome, of course, to stay here tonight. We'll talk again in the morning. I'll examine those papers tonight and see if they mean anything."

"Appreciate the hospitality, Stan."

Martin nodded. Then he turned abruptly. "You know, I wish there was something I could do. I don't like this mess any more than you do. And if I thought for one minute that one of my men was involved in it, you can bet I would court-martial him in an instant; but—"

"Look, Stan," Macomb said, "we're not trying to make trouble for you. But I got a man in my jailhouse caused, directly or indirectly, four murders. He didn't do it by hisself, neither. I want those other bastards before there's any more killing. I figure the army can handle its problems however it wants, but if one or more of your men is involved, I got to know that, and I got to know it soon. And by God, I *will* know it."

Martin nodded. "I understand. Let me show you your room. You'll have to double up. I hope you don't mind. There's not much in the way of luxury here." He climbed up the stairs and led them through the parlor to the rear of the house.

A modest room, two bunks arranged end to end along one wall, served as the guest quarters. Pointing to one end of the room, Martin said, "There's a linen closet. Whatever you need will be in there. Now, if you'll excuse me, I have some more work to do."

"Night, Stan, and thanks," Macomb said, clapping his friend on the shoulder.

"Good night, Mr. Slocum. I hope you'll think over what I said."

"I will, Colonel. Good night."

Martin left, and Macomb sat down on a bunk. "God, I'm tired," he said. "I'm not as young as I used to be, Slocum. I think I'll get some shut-eye. What about you?"

Slocum shrugged. "We're here. I think I might take a gander at the fort, see if anything interesting catches my eye."

"Don't you go stirrin' up trouble, Slocum. I don't want Stan Martin on my ass. I got enough trouble."

"Don't worry, Sheriff. I'll be careful. I don't want to call attention to our visit. If there is something here we ought to know about, the less noise we make, the more likely we are to stumble on it."

Macomb lay back on the bunk and Slocum walked back to the porch. He sat down and rolled a cigarette, lit it, and flicked the match into the dirt. He watched the thin trail of smoke rising from the match tip. The sun was about to set, and if it hadn't been for the field pieces fifty feet away in the center of the compound, he wouldn't have known he was at a military outpost.

He watched a handful of troopers playing cards on a rickety table in front of one of the barracks. For a minute, he thought about walking over to join them, but decided to keep to himself for a while. He had a few too many things to juggle in his own mind.

The sky turned pink as the sun slipped below the horizon. Dragging on the cigarette, he kept visualizing the faces of the five men who'd robbed the stage. He could see them clearly, especially the man with the shotgun, the one they called Pete, and Doak, the one who'd done all the shooting.

Pete had had a chance to kill him, even had the excuse, but he hadn't done it. Slocum wondered about that, wondered why one had killed so easily, with no provocation, and one had shown such restraint. How could men so different work together?

When the sky darkened, a couple of the card players excused themselves from the game and walked to the center of the compound. They spent several minutes in the darkness. Slocum could hear the steady thud of an ax, and the shriek of splitting timber. Then a tiny glow appeared. A minute later, Slocum could see the flicker of small flames. He watched the fire grow brighter.

A few of the men continued to play cards by lamplight. A figure on horseback appeared off to the left. It approached the fire and gradually became more defined. The horseman passed close to the flames. In the flickering illumination, Slocum recognized Chamberlain. The lieutenant spoke to the men tending the fire, then passed back into the shadows. Slocum got up and walked along the right side of the compound.

He couldn't see Chamberlain clearly now, but was able to track his progress past the lamplit windows along the opposite side of the fort. Chamberlain was in no hurry, and by the time he reached the far end of the camp, Slocum was directly across the compound from him.

The lieutenant tied his horse in front of a blocklike structure with no windows on the front. He went inside and closed the door. Slocum sprinted along the edge of the camp now, ducked between two buildings, and moved to the rear of the structure Chamberlain had just entered.

There was only one window on the rear of the building, and it was high on the wall. Dull light glowed behind the dusty panes. Slocum wanted to get a look inside. He found an abandoned length of timber at the base of the wall. Leaning it against the rough timbers of the building, he levered himself up. He could just barely see over the sill.

Chamberlain was sitting at a desk. Shelves in ranks filled the walls and some additional shelving stood in tiers in one half of the building. The shelves were anchored to the rafters to keep them from moving. In the narrow passages between shelves, the single lamp had no effect. Three or four men shuffled back and forth, uncrating supplies and storing them on the shelves. Chamberlain was busy checking a sheet of paper, apparently a bill of lading. The men called out goods and numbers as they opened one crate after another.

They must have been almost finished, because only three crates remained. Slocum held his precarious position while the last crates were opened, and the team of stockmen finally gathered around Chamberlain's desk.

Slocum nearly lost his balance when the fifth and last man moved toward the desk, clapping his hands to free them of dust. Even in the dim light, he could recognize Pete.

And he was wearing a uniform.

21

Slocum watched until the light went out. He had tried to listen to the conversation for nearly a half hour, but the voices were low and the storehouse was full of echoes which helped to obscure the words. When the men started to file out, Slocum dropped to the ground. His legs were cramped from the constant strain of keeping his balance on the timber. Moving the width of the building, he slipped down alongside it and waited at the corner.

None of the other men had been familiar. They weren't with the team that had held up the stage and they weren't the assailants who had dogged the footsteps of the witnesses back in Yuma.

But seeing Pete there, and in uniform, was another link in the chain connecting Chamberlain to the robbery. But the chain was incomplete. Pete could have acted without Chamberlain's knowledge. Nothing held the lieutenant accountable for the private lives of his men. But in his gut, Slocum knew the other links were there, somewhere. All he had to do was find them.

But where?

Pete was one of the first ones out. Slocum didn't know whether to follow him or follow Chamberlain. It was a coin

.toss, and Slocum was not afraid to take a chance. But if he went after Pete, he was almost certain to be seen. And if Chamberlain was *not* involved, then he might miss a chance to find one or more of the other robbers.

He wished he had rousted Macomb and brought him to the storehouse. They could have split up, one following the lieutenant and one following Pete. But he hadn't done it, and it was too late for second guesses.

When Chamberlain came out, he closed the door and locked it, then walked to his horse. For a moment, Slocum considered asking him point-blank about Pete, but it could ruin everything, so he bit his tongue and waited.

Chamberlain untied his horse, but didn't mount. Instead, he walked across the compound, leading his horse by its reins. At the post livery stable, he turned the mount over to a trooper, then made his way to his quarters. Slocum tagged along behind him, trying to hang in the shadows.

When the door closed behind Chamberlain, Slocum hotfooted it over to Colonel Martin's home. The front door was open, and he went to the back room. A lamp was burning, its flame turned way down. Macomb was asleep on his bunk. The sheriff hadn't even bothered to undress. He lay on the bunk with one arm trailing on the floor, his jaw slack and his barrel chest shuddering with every racking snore.

Slocum walked across the room and reached down to grab Macomb's shoulder and found himself staring into the mouth of a Colt .45.

Macomb was up and fully awake in a split second. "Jesus, man, don't sneak up on me like that," he said.

"I thought you were sleeping."

"I *was* sleeping. Sleep I need like a baby needs milk. What the hell's so important you have to interrupt it?"

"I found Pete."

"Pete who? What the hell are you jabberin' about?"

"Pete, the holdup man with the shotgun."

"What?"

"I saw him. Just now. He's here. In uniform."

"Are you sure?"

"No doubt in my mind. I watched him for close to an hour. He was working in the post supply room."

"Supply room? Didn't Stan say that's Chamberlain's responsibility?"

"Yeah, he did. And Chamberlain was there, too. They were uncrating supplies. I couldn't hear what they were talking about, even when they finished. Three or four other troopers were there, too. Unless they were all in on it, they probably weren't talking about the robbery, anyhow."

"You recognize any of the others?"

"Nope."

"They still there?"

Slocum shook his head. "Chamberlain went to his quarters and Pete's probably in his barracks. They may not know we're here, so there's no reason for them to spook. Yet."

Macomb started to get up. "We got to get Stan and get to the bottom of this business right now."

"I think we should wait."

"Wait? What for? Suppose they light out? We could lose them for good and all, then. That what you want?"

"You know it isn't. But I want *all* of them, and so do you, Sheriff. We'd be better off to be patient. There's a chance not all of them are in the army. We tip our hand now, and they get away clean. That's the last thing we want. Better to bide our time."

"We got to tell Colonel Martin. I can't go behind his back like that. He's got to be told."

"Will he go along?"

Macomb shrugged. "I guess he will. It won't cost him anything, so I don't see see why not. You sure they didn't see you?"

"I don't think so. I wouldn't bet my life on it, though."

"That may be exactly what you're betting, Slocum. Yours *and* mine."

"You got a better idea, I'd love to hear it."

Macomb shook his head. He started to pace, his hands folded behind his back. "Nope. I don't have a better idea. I'm not sure what you got is an idea at all, but since I don't have anything else, I guess I should just shut up." He dropped back to the bunk, ignoring the squeal of the wooden frame. "What I should do is go back to sleep."

"All right, then. We'll talk to Martin in the morning. I think we should look around some tomorrow and keep our eyes open, see what we can see."

Macomb looked skeptical. "Keep in mind that we have only four days before the trial. We can probably get Bradley, but if we're going to get the rest of them, it'll have to be soon. Otherwise, there won't be any witnesses. Miss Callahan is not going to stay in Yuma forever. And I know you'll be moving on soon."

"Let's worry about that later."

"Easy for you to say, Slocum." Macomb lay back on the bed and this time jerked a blanket over himself. "Get the lamp, would you?"

He was snoring again a moment later. But it wasn't that easy for Slocum. He turned down the lamp and lay on his own bunk. There had to be a way to smoke Chamberlain out of the nice, cozy hole he was hiding in, but Slocum was damned if he knew how. After an hour, he was no closer to a reasonable plan, and an hour after that, he was wondering whether it was time to give up.

But the thought of just walking away and letting four murderers go free, with no fewer than four innocent men already in the ground, and who knew how many others before that, made his blood boil. He drifted off to sleep, battling every minute, trying to haul himself back to wakefulness by sheer force of will. In the end, though, his tiredness overcame even that.

He was up again at dawn, after four hours of fitful sleep. He sat on the edge of his bunk listening to the rumble of Macomb's snoring. The sheriff finally shuddered awake around six. They heard reveille as they tidied the room, neither man in the mood to talk.

Slocum had his hand on the doorknob, when someone knocked.

"Let's rise and shine in there, gentlemen," Martin's voice boomed. "Breakfast!"

Slocum jerked the door open, and Martin nodded in approval. "Good to see civilians with a little discipline, Mr. Slocum. And I see even Vance is awake, or at least upright and mobile. We'll suspend judgment on the rest of it. You men ready for some chow?"

"We're ready for some information, Colonel."

Martin held up a hand. "Hold your horses, Mr. Slocum. There'll be plenty of time for that. I have some information for you. And I have some questions, too. But we can discuss it over breakfast. Let's move out."

Five minutes later they were seated around the breakfast table. Martin sensed Slocum's impatience, but he refused to be hurried. Not until everyone had a plate full of steak and eggs did he open the floor for discussion.

"Now, Mr. Slocum, let's hear what you have to say."

"You have an enlisted man here, name of Pete."

"Pete what? What's his last name?"

"I don't know, but I know he's here, because I saw him last night. He was working in your storeroom with Chamberlain."

"That would be Peter Margolin. Good man."

"Good man, hell. He was one of the men who held up the stage."

"Now, hold on just a minute, Slocum, you—"

"You hold on, Colonel. I saw him with my own eyes. He was packing a shotgun sawed off just ahead of the grip. You ever see him with a gun like that?"

"No, not to my knowledge."

"Well, he's got one. And since he was working with your lieutenant, I think we have the connection we need. So does Sheriff Macomb."

Martin looked at his old friend. "That right, Vance?"

Macomb nodded. " 'Fraid so, Stan."

Martin wiped his mouth with a linen napkin. "What do you want me to do?"

"I'm not sure, Stan. See, Slocum's concerned that some of the others might be your men, too. If Chamberlain is behind it, then he may be using some of his men. He knows about the payroll, so he can send them out knowing where and when to look for it."

"All right, let's say for a moment I accept that. If Chamberlain is not present, unless the others testify against him, I don't see what we can do."

"That's why we have to push him somehow," Slocum said. "We have to make him show his hand."

"Easier said than done, I'm afraid. He's not a man who frightens easily. Do you have any ideas?"

Slocum nodded. "Yes, I do. But we need more information. You have anybody here named Doak, first or last name?"

Martin nodded. "Doak Harbaugh. Got a bit of a temper, but he's never been in any serious trouble. Is he involved, too?"

"Is he one of Chamberlain's men?"

"Yes, as a matter of fact, he is. But you didn't answer my question."

"More than involved, Stan," Macomb said. "Sumbitch is the one who done the killin'. Least during the holdup. We don't know who killed the other two witnesses. Either Harbaugh or Margolin a good shot with a long gun?"

"Harbaugh is probably our best marksman."

"So," Slocum said, "a dead shot kills Tim Cartwright. A dead shot nearly kills me, and does kill one of your men by chance. You have a dead shot named Doak, and a man named Doak killed two men during the holdup of your payroll. The pieces coming together for you, Colonel?"

Martin sat there with his hands folded on the edge of the table. "Yes," he whispered, "they're coming together for me, Mr. Slocum. And there's more."

"Winslow's papers?"

Martin nodded. "Winslow's papers. It seems Mr. Winslow came to the conclusion that Walter Chamberlain was using his position as supply officer to steal everything from bacon to bullets. As near as I can piece it together from the scraps of information and the numbers in the papers, the theft began shortly after Chamberlain arrived. Winslow apparently discussed the shortages with Chamberlain, at least according to one of his letters to his employers, but didn't know who was responsible. He became suspicious when Chamberlain asked him to fudge the numbers in his audit."

"But Winslow never said anything to you?"

"No. I don't know whether he was bought off or frightened into silence. But he must have been keeping this information, either to protect himself or to threaten Chamberlain at some later date, maybe even blackmail. I don't know."

Slocum rubbed his chin. "That explains why they didn't kill him right away. They either knew or feared that he had the papers or had given them to someone for safekeeping. But they got edgy and decided to take a chance."

"Possibly."

"Look," Macomb said. "We can figure that part out later. Right now, we got to build a fire at one end of the burrow and see what comes out the other end. If I had a farm, I'd bet that one Lieutenant Walter Chamberlain will lead the parade. But we got to be certain."

"Every trap needs bait," Martin said.

Slocum patted Macomb on the shoulder. "And here we are," he said.

22

Macomb scratched his head. "I don't know, Slocum. You sure you want to take this risk? There's no need. You're a civilian. I got a job to do. But we can find some other way to do it. You're sticking your neck out pretty far, you know."

"Sheriff," Slocum said, "there is no other way and you know that as well as I do. We don't have time to be careful and we don't really have any way to do it except to make Chamberlain come after us."

Martin was still skeptical. "He might not take the bait, you know. There's nothing to prevent him from just sending Doak and some of the others after you. What then?"

"Then at least we get Doak and whoever else he sends. If we get enough of them, maybe one of them will give us Chamberlain."

"That's a big maybe, Slocum."

"It's the only maybe we have, Colonel. And I think it'll work. I think Chamberlain must be pretty close to the edge, now. His people have tried to get me more than once. They've tried to get Maggie Callahan, and they failed there, too. Most likely he'll take the bull by the horns, just to show the others how incompetent they are."

"All right, but you understand that I can't send any men after him. If I do that, he'll know he's been duped. He'll either run for cover or turn back before anything happens. Either way, we lose him. Once he knows we're on to him, he'll sit on his hands. Forever, if it takes that long."

"I understand."

"Tell me one thing, Slocum," Martin said. "Why are you doing this? What difference does it make to you? You don't know the men who were killed, you lost nothing of your own, and you don't even live here. And, God knows, you certainly have no love for the U.S. Army, unless I miss my guess."

"You're right on all counts, Colonel. But you forget one thing. I was there. I saw two men murdered in cold blood. I saw another young man gunned down from ambush. I saw the body of a fourth man, whose only real crime was that he talked too much and said too little. That's not a hangin' offense. And they tried to kill me, too. Any one of those things would be reason enough. Add them up, and you have all the reason you need."

Martin nodded. "I see. Since it's obvious you can't be talked out of this, the only thing that remains is to wish you Godspeed. And," he said, turning to Macomb, "Vance, you watch yourself. I'll be reassigned in another year or so. I don't feel like breaking in a new lawman in this area."

"You always were a lazy bastard, Stan," Macomb laughed.

"I'll wait an hour. Then I'll call Chamberlain in, tell him you have Winslow's papers and that Winslow is still alive. I'll tell him that Bradley is about to implicate his colleagues. Then I'll sit on my hands."

"You might actually fold them, and say a little prayer for us, Stan," Macomb suggested.

"Whatever influence I ever had with the Almighty has long since been exhausted, I'm afraid."

"You could always pull rank on Him," Macomb said.

"Get out of here. And be careful."

They were in the saddle five minutes later. They took a leisurely ride through the center of the oblong compound. Slocum spotted Pete out of the corner of his eye, but made no sign that he recognized the robber. Chamberlain was nowhere to be seen.

Without looking around, Slocum called attention to the gunman, warning Macomb not to make a sudden move. Turning his head and pretending to speak to Slocum, Macomb watched Pete disappear as soon as the two riders were past him.

"We may not need Stan to say anything," he said out of the corner of his mouth. "Old Pete has just scurried down the hole. Five'll get you ten he'll be whispering in Chamberlain's ear before we get out of sight of this place."

"No matter," Slocum said. "As long as they take the bait, I don't care how they know it's there."

It was already hot, and Slocum watched the sky as they rode. He knew they would have to preserve whatever strength their horses had. A prolonged chase that drained their mounts would put them at a real disadvantage, possibly a lethal one. It was best to set an easy pace, and stop often enough to let the animals conserve their energy.

They had stopped twice by noon, and there still had been no sign they were being followed. There had been no sign on either flank that anyone had tried to circle around in order to get ahead of them.

Dismounting at a shallow creek to water the horses, Macomb flopped on the bank upstream and filled his canteen. He hadn't said much for nearly an hour. It was apparent he was starting to lose his enthusiasm for Slocum's plan.

"Anything wrong, Sheriff?" Slocum asked.

"You know, Slocum, we been gone over four hours now, and they still haven't made a move. I don't even know if they're back there."

"They have to be."

"What makes you so sure?"

"Put yourself in Chamberlain's shoes, Sheriff. If you had been the brains behind the scheme, it led to murder, and you thought somebody knew about it, what would you do?"

Macomb shook his head. "Hell, I don't know what I'd do. I don't know what Chamberlain'd do, and neither do you, for that matter."

"Well, if it doesn't smoke him out, at least you have enough to go after him some other way, now."

"I do, huh? And I suppose I just go dig up Ralph Winslow and set him on the witness stand come Tuesday, that it?"

"It's early yet, Sheriff. The terrain isn't right, and Chamberlain, if he's smart—and I don't think there's any doubt about that—would want to make his move about midway between Yuma and Fort Hillman. Less chance of discovery."

"Take longer to find the bodies, too, wouldn't it?" Macomb grinned. "You know, Slocum, if I didn't know better, I'd think maybe you were some criminal, the way you figure this out. It's like you know exactly how they think. Hell, maybe you *are* a criminal."

Slocum backed away from the touchy subject. He knew he was wanted in half a dozen places. And he knew, too, that lawmen had ways of finding out such things. He wondered for a moment whether Macomb knew more than he was letting on. But it seemed unlikely. He hadn't been in Yuma that long, and there had been no real reason for Macomb to want to learn any more than he already knew.

Or had there?

Sweeping his binoculars across the flat expanse behind them, he searched from one corner of the horizon to the other.

"See anything?"

"Nope."

"And you ain't gonna, Slocum. I'm telling you. This is a long shot, and it ain't gonna work."

"We can't afford to think that now, Sheriff. Because if it *does* work, we want to be ready. Doak Harbaugh won't miss me the next time. Not if I give him half a chance."

Macomb nodded. "You're right. I know that. But I'm getting impatient. Always was, and now it's getting worse." Shielding his eyes from the brilliant glare, he scanned the terrain ahead of them. A range of low mountains began to ripple the ground a mile or two ahead. It was nearly ten miles through winding valleys and shallow ravines. Then the land flattened out again almost all the way to Yuma. It looked nearly the way a rug would look if somebody had bunched it in the middle, the low folds drooping over one another and doubling back.

For an ambush, it was the best choice. But if Chamberlain didn't see them head into the convoluted terrain, he'd never find them. That meant he had to be within sight of them when they reached it—or already there, waiting, and watching as they approached.

"You about ready?" Slocum asked, looping the field glasses over his saddle horn.

"I been ready."

Slocum swung up into the saddle. He looked back one more time, shielding his eyes, but not bothering with the binoculars. Still no sign of pursuit.

Fifteen minutes later, the ground began to rise noticeably. Slocum looked back again, knowing that, as they climbed, they would be visible from farther away. It dawned on him then that Chamberlain would be aware of that, and there would have been no need for him to get too close. He could hang back and wait for Slocum to commit himself to one of a handful of possible routes.

And he would have to commit himself very soon. In fifteen minutes they would be heading into a steep-sided valley. From that point on, the route was predictable and all but inevitable, unless a rider were trying to throw off someone on his tail.

But Slocum didn't have that option. He *wanted* to be followed, so he and Macomb were locking themselves in once they entered the valley.

Slocum slowed as the shallow mouth opened to swallow him. He used the glasses again, and this time he saw something. It wasn't much, and it sure wasn't clear, but he knew what it meant.

"Riders coming, Sheriff," he said. He pointed toward the faint cloud of dust almost two miles behind them.

Macomb squinted against the sun. "I see 'em. How many, do you figure?"

"Can't tell. Five, six, I'd guess."

"We can't afford to guess, Slocum. Not now. If those men are who we think they are, they're comin' to shoot us dead. We got to know."

"We'll have to wait until they get closer, Sheriff."

"Not long, boy. Don't wait too long. Two against six is already long odds. Especially if one of them is a sharpshooter. And I know Stan Martin well enough to know he don't exaggerate a thing like that. This Harbaugh is gonna be our number-one problem, Slocum."

"We'll handle it, Sheriff. But we have to let them get close. Right now they're nibbling. We have to make sure they take the bait before we set the hook."

"I can feel that bastard's sights on me, right smack dab in the middle of my back. That hook set enough for you?"

"Not, yet, Sheriff. Not just yet. They have to come into the valley if we're going to have a chance. It's the only cover for miles, and the only chance we have to pin them down long enough to pick them off one by one."

"I just hope you ain't biting off more than you can swallow."

"We'll know soon enough, Sheriff."

They pushed on another quarter mile. The sides of the valley were much steeper now. Covered with loose, dry dirt and studded with rocks, they seemed to be held in place by columns of rock showing through the thin soil like ribs on a hungry dog.

Ahead, the sides grew even more precipitous, and in a couple of hundred yards, they would be too steep to permit ascent on horseback. If Chamberlain and his men managed to get to either ridge, they would have the edge in numbers and control of the high ground.

The riders were closing fast now, no longer concerned about being spotted. They were pushing their mounts flat out. The dust cloud boiling up behind them drifted off to the east, thinning slowly and growing more and more transparent before it vanished altogether. They were less than half a mile away. Not far from rifle range.

It was time to make a move.

23

"Split up," Slocum shouted. "You take the right and I'll take the left."

Macomb waved and turned his horse, spurring it up the stony slope. The loose footing made going difficult. Slocum watched for a few seconds as the horse floundered through the skidding soil, then urged his own horse toward the opposite slope.

The big chestnut struggled across the scree at an angle, losing ground and nearly stumbling every few steps as the scree gave way beneath its hooves. Looking back, he saw the riders charge into the narrowing valley. So far, there hadn't been a shot fired, but that would change very quickly.

As he neared the top of the treacherous slope, Slocum glanced down again and saw six men, all in cavalry uniforms, break into two groups. Three plunged up the far slope and three barreled up the hill toward him.

Slocum urged the chestnut up and over the ridgeline, then dismounted. Jerking his Winchester from its boot, he smacked the chestnut on the rump and shouted to send it on into the jumbled rocks and mesquite studding the tablelike hilltop.

Gunfire broke out somewhere behind him and, as he worked his way back toward the ridgeline, he spotted three of Chamberlain's men on foot, racing through the loose dirt on the far slope. They were firing at random, more to pin Macomb down than to actually hit him.

The three men below started firing their own weapons, and Slocum was forced to press himself into the dry soil to keep out of the line of fire. He needed cover in order to be able to look down the slope and keep track of his pursuers. A clump of tangled mesquite jutted out of the ridgeline at an angle about thirty feet to his left.

Skittering back from the ridge a few feet, Slocum got into a crouch and zigzagged toward the mesquite and hit the ground just ahead of a sharp volley.

Things were moving too fast for him to get a fix on the men below. He didn't even know whether Chamberlain himself was there. His three assailants had taken cover behind the slabs of shattered stone littering the slope. It was easier for him to see Macomb's pursuers than his own.

The men were in uniform, which meant they were confident, maybe even reckless. But it also meant that they had no intention of leaving either him or Macomb alive. They were here to exterminate them both. Should anyone happen along, the uniforms were sufficient authority to send them packing. Army business. Mind your own. And no one would argue.

Slocum used the binoculars to scan the far slope. He found the three men easily, but none of their faces could be seen. The only thing he knew for certain was that there was no one wearing a lieutenant's insignia. If Chamberlain was here, he was on Slocum's side or he was out of uniform.

The rocks below offered reasonable cover, and Slocum used the glasses to check the most likely spots, positions that would offer protection from the ridge, but some freedom to maneuver and to fire without undue exposure.

A gunshot cracked below, but the bullet hit nothing, and Slocum dropped the glasses to get a broader view of the slope. The gunman was already back behind his cover. The sun was just past the meridian, and the heat was continuing to rise. Looking off toward the mouth of the valley, Slocum could see the air shimmer as if a current of water were rising to the sky.

A siege could last till nightfall. If that happened, all bets were off. The balance would shift to the pursuers. Defensive positions like his and Macomb's were only useful if you could keep your opponents pinned. Darkness would give them the freedom to move without being seen. Then numbers would matter, and the weight of numbers was in Chamberlain's favor.

He had to do something.

Scanning the far slope, he found the easiest target of the three. It was a long shot, but he'd made longer. If Macomb was alert, it might pay off even if he missed. If the gunman were flushed from his cover, he might expose himself to Macomb's gun. It was worth a try.

He picked the man farthest up the slope. Crouched behind a squarish boulder, he was about seventy feet below the ridge where Macomb lay. Sighting carefully, Slocum drew a bead and squeezed the trigger. The carbine bucked, and he saw a puff of dust kick up just a couple of inches below the crouching form.

The gunman turned. His face was just a blur on the bright slope. But he didn't move. Slocum swept his eyes across the slope below him. No one had showed himself, and he turned his attention back to the target.

He peered through the glasses at him. It wasn't Pete and it wasn't Doak. The face didn't look at all familiar. It could have been one of the men who tried to break into Maggie's room, but he couldn't be sure. But for the moment, it didn't really matter.

The man was watching him now, trying to cut down

his profile by lying on his side. The nearest cover from Slocum's gun was twenty-five feet away. If Macomb was alert, he'd be watching, ready to fire at the first hint of movement.

Sighting in again, Slocum compensated for his previous error. The gunman shouted something Slocum didn't catch, but the result was immediate. All three men on Slocum's side opened up at once. The sudden furious hail drove him deep into the loose dirt, and he pressed his cheek to the ground. Waiting for the gunfire to die down, he heard a more distant crack.

Macomb had gotten the idea. His shot sent the men below diving for cover and Slocum peeked over the ridge. His target was still there. Sighting again, he squeezed the trigger. This time he was on the money. He saw the man jerk, then tumble to one side. He lay flat, one arm curled over his shoulder. With the other, he emptied his pistol in Slocum's direction, wasting ammunition and leaving himself the difficult proposition of having to reload with a bad arm.

Slocum sighted once more. When the carbine slammed back into his shoulder, he knew it was a good shot. He watched as the gunman bucked as if he'd been stung, then curled his body into a near circle and lay still.

The odds were getting better.

Another explosion of gunfire ripped up the hill, plowing furrows in the loose dirt along the slope as Slocum crept back away from the edge. Extending the Winchester over his head, he rolled to the left three times. There was no cover, but if he moved quickly, he'd have a couple of seconds of surprise.

Scurrying back to the ridgeline, he saw one of the men below him scramble to his feet and charge up the slope. Slocum fired quickly, wide, but freezing the man in his tracks for a split second. He'd seen the face before. One of the holdup men. The hesitation was all Slocum needed. He had another shell jacked home and squeezed off a

second shot, shooting from a crouch, and the man fell
backward, sliding downhill a few feet with his arms flailing
and clawing at the sand and gravel.

He rolled onto his stomach then, knowing he was still
under Slocum's sights, and hauled himself downhill. He
looked like a swimmer who'd run out of water and couldn't
stop his stroke. Slocum fired once more. This time, the
bullet did the ultimate damage.

"Slocum!" The voice exploded as suddenly as a gunshot.
He recognized Chamberlain, but ignored the call.

"Slocum, you can't get away. You know that. You rebs
are all the same. You don't know how to fight. You run like
rabbits when it gets rough. But you're flat out of running
room, Reb."

He knew Chamberlain was going to try to bait him,
and he ignored it. Getting mad would just play into the
lieutenant's hands. He thought about trading insults, maybe
getting Chamberlain so angry he'd make a mistake. But
he'd already done that. Chamberlain was desperate now.
The lieutenant had opened a box he couldn't close, no
matter how much he wanted to.

It was better to let him stew. Already, the odds had
shifted in Slocum's favor. On either slope they were down
to two to one. Not great, but a hell of a lot better than
three to one. But one of the remaining four was Doak
Harbaugh, and that made a difference Slocum couldn't
calculate. He wished to God he knew where Harbaugh
was. Concentrate on him, take him out, and the game was
all but over.

But there was only one way, and that was too risky. He
could expose himself, minimally, and draw Harbaugh's
fire. The marksman would try a shot none of the others would bother with. But if he cut it too close, and
if Harbaugh was as good as Martin had said, he'd be a
dead man.

He needed an edge, but he'd be damned if he knew where
to get it. Creeping back to the ridgeline, he used the glasses

again. He could only get high enough to see the men on Macomb's side of the ravine. One had his back to him, and one, the only one whose face he could see, was a man he'd never seen before. If he could get the other man to turn, he'd know where Harbaugh was. It wasn't much, but when there wasn't much, you took what you could get.

Grabbing two rocks, each the size of his head, he set the Winchester between them, using the rocks to pin the barrel of the carbine in place. Sighting in, he pushed a mound of dirt up under the stock. His angle was too steep now, but that's what he wanted. Resighting, he pressed the carbine into the soft dirt.

When the gunman looking up at Macomb's position was dead center, he found him in the glasses, keeping his finger on the Winchester's trigger. He might have only a split second, and it might not work, but he wanted to know, and this was the only way.

With the back of the gunman's head in the field glasses, he pulled the trigger. The shot went low and left, but the man snapped his head around. Not long, but long enough. It was Pete Margolin. That meant Harbaugh was on *his* side.

Macomb opened fire suddenly, getting into a crouch and jerking round after round into his rifle's chamber. But when he was done, the two men were still there. Slocum watched through the glasses as Macomb dropped down and out of sight.

Almost as suddenly as the firing had stopped, as if he had been waiting for just that moment, the second man on the slope scrambled to his feet and charged toward Macomb's position. Slocum watched helplessly, waiting for the sheriff to open fire, but nothing happened. Maybe the rifle was jammed, maybe Macomb had been hit. But a stationary target was not the same as a man pounding uphill. All Slocum could do was wait and hope.

Slocum shouted, "Vance, look out!" but his words would

be meaningless sounds by the time they reached the sheriff, assuming he could even hear them. He saw Pete Margolin get to his feet and race after the charging gunman. Closing the gap in half a dozen strides, Margolin tackled the other man and hauled him to the ground. They rolled over and over in a tangle of limbs.

Macomb popped up then, his carbine in his hand. He saw what was happening below and started down the slope.

A shot cracked from just below Slocum, and he saw Macomb stumble. He couldn't tell whether the sheriff had been hit or just tripped. Margolin and the other man were thrashing around fifty yards below, and Macomb lay spread-eagled on the sand, trying to stop his own head-long slide.

Another rifle shot exploded below, and a puff of dust kicked up just inches from Macomb's head.

Slocum got to his feet and charged downhill.

Charmberlain saw him, but Harbaugh must have been intent on the sheriff. The lieutenant opened fire, his head raised just above an outcropping of rock.

Slocum fired from the hip, his shot scattering sparks and rock slivers just to the right of Chamberlain's surprised face. Then Chamberlain disappeared.

Margolin lay on his back now and the second gunman was scrambling back up the slope. Thunder clapped across the ravine, and Slocum saw the gunman go down. Macomb was still facedown in the dirt. It took Slocum a second to realize what had happened. Margolin had used his sawed-off shotgun on his own man.

Margolin got unsteadily to his feet and started toward the still form of the sheriff. Harbaugh must have realized what had happened. His rifle barked, and Margolin went down.

The shout burst from Slocum before his brain had even formed the words. "Doooak! You bastard!"

Harbaugh turned then as Slocum loped down the hillside toward him. He was bringing his rifle around at the instant

Slocum leaped onto a boulder and launched himself through the air. The impact sent both men rolling head over heels. Harbaugh was clawing at the ground, conscious of the increasing distance from his rifle.

Slocum spread his arms wide and plowed the dirt with his chin.

But he stopped.

24

Slocum's rifle lay uphill, not far from Harbaugh's. Doak
had stopped between him and both rifles. Harbaugh started
to scramble back up the hill as Slocum reached for his Colt
Navy, but the pistol had come out of its holster. It was gone.
He felt a rock the size of his fist digging into his back. As he
got to his knees, he closed his fist over the rock and raised
it in his right hand.

Chamberlain was coming toward him, slipping and sliding downhill, a Colt in his fist. His face was bleeding from
several cuts where stone slivers or bullet fragments had torn
at the flesh. The lieutenant had one eye covered with his
other hand and when he fired, the shot went wild. Ducking
to one side, Slocum spun around, straightened, and threw
the rock as hard as he could.

Chamberlain saw it coming and tried to dodge, but the
stone caught him a glancing blow high on the shoulder.
He went down on one knee, grabbing at the shoulder and
Slocum bulled uphill and charged into him, knocking the
lieutenant to the ground. Chamberlain cursed and tried to
bring his pistol to bear, but Slocum caught hold of the
gun hand and bent the wrist back. Something popped, and

Chamberlain let out a howl. The gun fell to the ground, landing barrel first in the soft dirt.

Slocum snatched at it, cracked it sharply against Chamberlain's skull. The stunned cavalryman fell to his knees. Slapping his thigh with the gun, Slocum tried to clear the dirt clogged in the barrel. Harbaugh had nearly reached the rifles and Slocum was too far away to catch him. He rapped the gun again against his heel, saw the clods of dirt fall free, and swung the pistol just as Doak levered a shell into his carbine's chamber.

Slocum dove to the ground and rolled to his right. He heard the sharp report of the rifle and the whine of a slug glancing off a rock somewhere behind him. Harbaugh worked the lever again and was resighting just as Chamberlain got to his feet. Armed only with a knife now, the lieutenant charged toward Slocum. He hurled himself through the air, shouting for Doak to hold his fire.

Chamberlain was a big man, and he was strong. His weight pinned Slocum to the ground for a moment, and he brought the knife high over his head. Slocum saw the brilliant glint of sunlight on the polished steel and heaved with his legs. Chamberlain lost his balance for a moment, and stabbed the blade at the ground to try and regain it.

With Chamberlain on top of him, Slocum was having difficulty breathing. He felt his strength beginning to fade. Fifty feet away, he saw Doak Harbaugh's boots as the marksman waited for the outcome of the struggle.

Slocum heaved one more time and this time got his gun hand free. Doak was racing downhill now, and Slocum aimed and fired. The slug caught Harbaugh in the chest, but he kept on coming, his carbine wavering but still pointed in Slocum's direction.

Chamberlain sliced awkwardly with the big knife gripped in his left hand, and Slocum locked his free hand on the lieutenant's wrist, letting the gun fall to the ground.

Chamberlain's left hand lacked the strength and control of his right, but the blade was razor sharp, and even a casual slice could sever an artery. Twisting the arm, Slocum pushed sideways, finally succeeding in tossing Chamberlain free. Reaching out to break his fall with the injured right hand, Chamberlain screamed when his full weight put pressure on the broken wrist.

Harbaugh tried to keep his balance, but stumbled and sat down. He was weaving from side to side, still trying to aim the carbine. Snatching at the pistol, Slocum scrambled away from Chamberlain and fired again. This time, the bullet caught Harbaugh high on the shoulder. Slocum heard the crack of breaking bone, and Harbaugh went over on his back. He lost his grip on the rifle, and it lay between his legs.

Slocum turned just as Chamberlain got to his feet again, still clutching the knife in his left hand.

"You bastard," he cursed. "I'm going to kill you, Slocum. Kill you like a goddamned dog. I'm going to cut your throat and watch you bleed to death."

Slocum shook his head. "You're not going to kill anybody, Chamberlain. You're going to hang."

"The hell I am." The lieutenant rushed toward him, the knife extended before him. Slocum slipped to one side, almost losing his balance as Chamberlain rushed past. He had the pistol in his hand, but he didn't want to use it. He wanted Chamberlain to come to trial, whether a court-martial or a civilian court, he didn't give a damn. He was vaguely aware that, somewhere behind him, Harbaugh was still within reach of his rifle, but he couldn't take his eyes off Chamberlain to see what Harbaugh was up to.

And Chamberlain was determined. He charged again, forcing Slocum to back away, still holding the Colt out in front of him, and still unwilling to pull the trigger. But he cocked the hammer, hoping that would slow Chamberlain down. It didn't seem to matter. The lieutenant was determined that one of them would take his last breath before it was all over.

Slocum shook his head, dodged a second rush, and fired. He aimed low, and the bullet caught Chamberlain above the knee. The bullet struck bone and the lieutenant went down hard, letting go of the knife to clutch at the wounded leg.

But he didn't give up. Moaning in agony, he retrieved the blade, then dragged himself toward Slocum, stabbing the knife into the ground and using it to pull himself forward. Again and again he clawed at the ground, while Slocum just kept backing away.

Chamberlain was whimpering, as much in frustration as in pain.

Backing rapidly downhill, Slocum watched the lieutenant change direction, sliding now as much as crawling. But he kept on coming. The wounded leg was bleeding heavily, leaving a trail of bloody sand behind at the bottom of a shallow rut. Glancing over his shoulder, he saw someone moving on the valley floor, but he couldn't afford to take his eyes off Chamberlain long enough to see who it was.

"Sheriff, that you?"

He looked back a second time. He thought he recognized Macomb's shirt. But there were two figures now, one limping. In desperation, Chamberlain threw the knife. It fell pathetically short, skittered on the loose dirt a few feet, and lay still, shining in the sunlight.

"Slocum!"

The shout stunned him, and he turned to see Harbaugh grinning at him, propped on his elbows, the carbine aimed dead center. He moved to the right, and the sudden shift threw Harbaugh off for a moment. He was having trouble focusing his eyes and keeping his aim steady.

"You had no business messing in this, Slocum," Harbaugh said. His voice sounded weak, and his eyes kept opening and closing. "You should have kept your nose out."

Dodging again, Slocum raised the Colt at the same instant the carbine cracked. He felt something tear at his shoulder, a hot, stabbing pain, as he went down on one knee. He fired the Colt twice, and hit Harbaugh both times, once in the head and once in the back as the marksman slumped forward.

It was over.

Ignoring Chamberlain, who was still cursing and whimpering, he turned to look downhill. Vance Macomb had started up the slope. He was holding his side, and Slocum could see a bright smear of blood midway between Macomb's waist and shoulder.

"You all right?" the sheriff called.

Slocum nodded. "I'll live."

"Me, too."

The second figure appeared again as Macomb drifted to one side. Further downhill, Pete Margolin limped uphill, wincing with every step. Slocum looked beyond him, and Macomb saw the glance.

"He's all right," the sheriff said. "Had enough killing. Saved my life with that hogleg of his. Ugly what it does to a man, but I ain't complainin'."

"I guess you got your witness, then, Sheriff."

"Sounds like you don't aim to hang around for the trial."

"Only if you need me. But I don't guess you do, now."

"You're right. If he testifies." Macomb cocked a thumb over his shoulder at the limping Margolin. "But suppose he changes his mind. What do I do then?"

Margolin had heard the exchange. He was close enough now to say, "I won't change my mind, Sheriff."

"Maybe not, but I'd like Slocum to stay on, all the same. No offense."

Slocum gave in reluctantly. "All right, Sheriff. I'll stay. Until the trial."

"That's all I'm askin'." He pointed toward Chamberlain. "He gonna live long enough to stretch a rope?"

"He'll live."

"That'll be a pure pleasure to see. I ain't much for hangin's, but I think I'll make an exception in his case."

25

Maggie closed the door. She held a hairbrush in her right hand and swiped absently at her curls. "I was afraid you weren't going to come back," she said.

"I told you I'd be careful."

She shrugged. "Men always say that. And they never are. You're like that, Slocum. You're reckless, and you don't care."

"Maybe women like to think that way. Maybe that's why men are reckless. And maybe men do what they can to meet the expectations."

She shook her head. "No, that's not it. But I'm glad you're safe." She saw the bloodstained sleeve. He saw her eyes linger there a moment, but didn't mention it. Neither did Maggie.

"Doak is dead," he said.

"I'm glad."

"What now?" he asked.

She let the brush fall and came toward him, her arms extended. He stayed still, letting her encircle him. She rested her head on his shoulder, and he reached out to tangle his fingers in her hair. "I don't know."

"You'll stay for the trial?"

She nodded. "Yes. Will you?"

"That's up to the sheriff."

"And if he says there's no need?"

"I don't know."

"Then we don't have very much time, do we?"

He shook his head. "No."

She let her arms fall and stepped back. She gave him a strange smile, tinged with sadness and regret. Her head bobbed and she said, "I understand." She reached for her buttons and started to undo them.

He followed her lead. She watched his face the whole time, and when they were undressed, she reached out a hand, curled his fingers in hers, and moved toward the bed. She didn't pull him, because she didn't have to. They were moving together.

She lay on her back and he lay beside her, on one hip. He let his hands wander over her skin, and she was amazed at how light his touch was. It felt to her almost as if he had already gone. It was like the memory of fingertips tracing a vein here, outlining the curve of a breast there.

She didn't move. He was already hard, and when he was ready, he reached down to part her legs, then got on his knees between them. As he started to enter her, she let the tip of her tongue moisten her lips. He thought she was going to speak, but she didn't. Then she nodded, and he slid all the way home. Her hands closed over his hips and held him still for a long moment. She closed her eyes then, and he started to move.

He watched her face, the perfect features bronzed by the lamplight. He thought he saw a glistening bead in the corner of her eye. For a little while, he didn't feel quite so alone. But he knew that wouldn't last.

GILES TIPPETTE

Author of the bestselling WILSON YOUNG
SERIES, BAD NEWS, and CROSS FIRE

is back with his most exciting
Western adventure yet!

JAILBREAK

Time is running out for Justa Williams, owner of the Half-
Moon Ranch in West Texas. His brother Norris is being
held in a Mexican jail, and neither bribes nor threats can
free him.

Now, with the help of a dozen kill-crazy Mexican *banditos*,
Justa aims to blast Norris out. But the worst is yet to come:
a hundred-mile chase across the Mexican desert with fifty
federales in hot pursuit.

The odds of reaching the Texas border are a million to nothing . . . and if the Williams brothers don't watch their backs,
the road to freedom could turn into the road to hell!

Turn the page for an exciting preview of
JAILBREAK by Giles Tippette

On sale now, wherever Jove Books are sold!

At supper Norris, my middle brother, said, "I think we got some trouble on that five thousand acres down on the border near Laredo."

He said it serious, which is the way Norris generally says everything. I quit wrestling with the steak Buttercup, our cook, had turned into rawhide and said, "What are you talking about? How could we have trouble on land lying idle?"

He said, "I got word from town this afternoon that a telegram had come in from a friend of ours down there. He says we got some kind of squatters taking up residence on the place."

My youngest brother, Ben, put his fork down and said, incredulously, "*That* five thousand acres? Hell, it ain't nothing but rocks and cactus and sand. Why in hell would anyone want to squat on that worthless piece of nothing?"

Norris just shook his head. "I don't know. But that's what the telegram said. Came from Jack Cole. And if anyone ought to know what's going on down there it would be him."

I thought about it and it didn't make a bit of sense. I was Justa Williams, and my family, my two brothers

and myself and our father, Howard, occupied a considerable ranch called the Half-Moon down along the Gulf
of Mexico in Matagorda County, Texas. It was some of
the best grazing land in the state and we had one of the
best herds of purebred and crossbred cattle in that part of
the country. In short we were pretty well-to-do.

But that didn't make us any the less ready to be stolen
from, if indeed that was the case. The five thousand acres
Norris had been talking about had come to us through a
trade our father had made some years before. We'd never
made any use of the land, mainly because, as Ben had
said, it was pretty worthless and because it was a good
two hundred miles from our ranch headquarters. On a few
occasions we'd bought cattle in Mexico and then used the
acreage to hold small groups on while we made up a herd.
But other than that, it lay mainly forgotten.

I frowned. "Norris, this doesn't make a damn bit of sense.
Right after supper send a man into Blessing with a return
wire for Jack asking him if he's certain. What the hell kind
of squatting could anybody be doing on that land?"

Ben said, "Maybe they're raisin' watermelons." He
laughed.

I said, "They could raise melons, but there damn sure
wouldn't be no water in them."

Norris said, "Well, it bears looking into." He got up,
throwing his napkin on the table. "I'll go write out that
telegram."

I watched him go, dressed, as always, in his town clothes.
Norris was the businessman in the family. He'd been sent
down to the University at Austin and had got considerable
learning about the ins and outs of banking and land deals
and all the other parts of our business that didn't directly
involve the ranch. At the age of twenty-nine I'd been the
boss of the operation a good deal longer than I cared to
think about. It had been thrust upon me by our father when
I wasn't much more than twenty. He'd said he wanted
me to take over while he was still strong enough to help
me out of my mistakes and I reckoned that was partly true.

But it had just seemed that after our mother had died the life had sort of gone out of him. He'd been one of the earliest settlers, taking up the land not long after Texas had become a republic in 1845. I figured all the years of fighting Indians and then Yankees and scalawags and carpetbaggers and cattle thieves had taken their toll on him. Then a few years back he'd been nicked in the lungs by a bullet that should never have been allowed to head his way and it had thrown an extra strain on his heart. He was pushing seventy and he still had plenty of head on his shoulders, but mostly all he did now was sit around in his rocking chair and stare out over the cattle and land business he'd built. Not to say that I didn't go to him for advice when the occasion demanded. I did, and mostly I took it.

Buttercup came in just then and sat down at the end of the table with a cup of coffee. He was near as old as Dad and almost completely worthless. But he'd been one of the first hands that Dad had hired and he'd been kept on even after he couldn't sit a horse anymore. The problem was he'd elected himself cook, and that was the sorriest day our family had ever seen. There were two Mexican women hired to cook for the twelve riders we kept full-time, but Buttercup insisted on cooking for the family.

Mainly, I think, because he thought he was one of the family. A notion we could never completely dissuade him from.

So he sat there, about two days of stubble on his face, looking as scrawny as a pecked-out rooster, sweat running down his face, his apron a mess. He said, wiping his forearm across his forehead, "Boy, it shore be hot in there. You boys shore better be glad you ain't got no business takes you in that kitchen."

Ben said, in a loud mutter, "I wish you didn't either."

Ben, at twenty-five, was easily the best man with a horse or a gun that I had ever seen. His only drawback was that he was hotheaded and he tended to act first and think later. That ain't a real good combination for someone that could go on the prod as fast as Ben. When I had argued with Dad about taking over as boss, suggesting instead that Norris, with his education, was a much better choice, Dad had simply said, "Yes, in some ways. But he can't handle Ben. You can. You can handle Norris, too. But none of them can handle you."

Well, that hadn't been exactly true. If Dad had wished it I would have taken orders from Norris even though he was two years younger than me. But the logic in Dad's line of thinking had been that the Half-Moon and our cattle business was the lodestone of all our businesses and only I could run that. He had been right. In the past I'd imported purebred Whiteface and Hereford cattle from up North, bred them to our native Longhorns and produced cattle that would bring twice as much at market as the horse-killing, all-bone, all-wild Longhorns. My neighbors had laughed at me at first, claiming those square little purebreds would never make it in our Texas heat. But they'd been wrong and, one by one, they'd followed the example of the Half-Moon.

Buttercup was setting up to take off on another one of his long-winded harangues about how it had been in the "old days" so I quickly got up, excusing myself, and went into the big office we used for sitting around in as well as a place of business. Norris was at the desk composing his telegram so I poured myself out a whiskey and sat down. I didn't want to hear about any trouble over some worthless five thousand acres of borderland. In fact I didn't want to hear about any troubles of any kind. I was just two weeks short of getting married, married to a lady I'd been courting off and on for five years, and I was mighty anxious that nothing come up to interfere with our plans. Her name was Nora Parker and her daddy owned and run the general mercantile in our nearest town, Blessing. I'd almost lost her once before to a Kansas City drummer. She'd finally gotten tired of waiting on me, waiting until the ranch didn't occupy all my time, and almost run off with a smooth-talking Kansas City drummer that called on her daddy in the harness trade. But she'd come to her senses in time and got off the train in Texarkana and returned home.

But even then it had been a close thing. I, along with my men and brothers and help from some of our neighbors, had been involved with stopping a huge herd of illegal cattle being driven up from Mexico from crossing our range and infecting our cattle with tick fever which could have wiped us all out. I tell you it had been a bloody business. We'd lost four good men and had to kill at least a half dozen on the other side. Fact of the business was I'd come about as close as I ever had to getting killed myself, and that was going some for the sort of rough-and-tumble life I'd led.

Nora had almost quit me over it, saying she just couldn't take the uncertainty. But in the end, she'd stuck by me. That had been the year before, 1896, and I'd convinced her that civilized law was coming to the country, but until it did, we that had been there before might have to take things into our own hands from time to time.

She'd seen that and had understood. I loved her and she loved me and that was enough to overcome any of the troubles we were still likely to encounter from day to day.

So I was giving Norris a pretty sour look as he finished his telegram and sent for a hired hand to ride it into Blessing, seven miles away. I said, "Norris, let's don't make a big fuss about this. That land ain't even crossed my mind in at least a couple of years. Likely we got a few Mexican families squatting down there and trying to scratch out a few acres of corn."

Norris gave me his businessman's look. He said, "It's our land, Justa. And if we allow anyone to squat on it for long enough or put up a fence they can lay claim. That's the law. My job is to see that we protect what we have, not give it away."

I sipped at my whiskey and studied Norris. In his town clothes he didn't look very impressive. He'd inherited more from our mother than from Dad so he was not as wide-shouldered and slim-hipped as Ben and me. But I knew him to be a good, strong, dependable man in any kind of fight. Of course he wasn't that good with a gun, but then Ben and I weren't all that good with books like he was. But I said, just to jolly him a bit, "Norris, I do believe you are running to suet. I may have to put you out with Ben working the horse herd and work a little of that fat off you."

Naturally it got his goat. Norris had always envied Ben and me a little. I was just over six foot and weighed right around one hundred and ninety. I had inherited my daddy's big hands and big shoulders. Ben was almost a copy of me except he was about a size smaller. Norris said, "I weigh the same as I have for the last five years. If it's any of your business."

I said, as if I was being serious, "Must be them sack suits you wear. What they do, pad them around the middle?"

He said, "Why don't you just go to hell."

After he'd stomped out of the room I got the bottle of whiskey and an extra glass and went down to Dad's room. It had been one of his bad days and he'd taken to bed right after lunch. Strictly speaking he wasn't supposed to have no whiskey, but I watered him down a shot every now and then and it didn't seem to do him no harm.

He was sitting up when I came in the room. I took a moment to fix him a little drink, using some water out of his pitcher, then handed him the glass and sat down in the easy chair by the bed. I told him what Norris had reported and asked what he thought.

He took a sip of his drink and shook his head. "Beats all I ever heard," he said. "I took that land in trade for a bad debt some fifteen, twenty years ago. I reckon I'd of been money ahead if I'd of hung on to the bad debt. That land won't even raise weeds, well as I remember, and Noah was in on the last rain that fell on the place."

We had considerable amounts of land spotted around the state as a result of this kind of trade or that. It was Norris's business to keep up with their management. I was just bringing this to Dad's attention more out of boredom and impatience for my wedding day to arrive than anything else.

I said, "Well, it's a mystery to me. How you feeling?"

He half smiled. "Old." Then he looked into his glass. "And I never liked watered whiskey. Pour me a dollop of the straight stuff in here."

I said, "Now, Howard. You know—"

He cut me off. "If I wanted somebody to argue with I'd send for Buttercup. Now do like I told you."

I did, but I felt guilty about it. He took the slug of whiskey down in one pull. Then he leaned his head back on the pillow and said, "Aaaaah. I don't give a damn what that horse doctor says, ain't nothing makes a man feel as good inside as a shot of the best."

I felt sorry for him laying there. He'd always led just the kind of life he wanted—going where he wanted, doing what he wanted, having what he set out to get. And now he was reduced to being a semi-invalid. But one thing that showed the strength that was still in him was that you *never* heard him complain. He said, "How's the cattle?"

I said, "They're doing all right, but I tell you we could do with a little of Noah's flood right now. All this heat and no rain is curing the grass off way ahead of time. If it doesn't let up we'll be feeding hay by late September, early October. And that will play hell on our supply. Could be we won't have enough to last through the winter. Norris thinks we ought to sell off five hundred head or so, but the market is doing poorly right now. I'd rather chance the weather than take a sure beating by selling off."

He sort of shrugged and closed his eyes. The whiskey was relaxing him. He said, "You're the boss."

"Yeah," I said. "Damn my luck."

I wandered out of the back of the house. Even though it was nearing seven o'clock of the evening it was still good and hot. Off in the distance, about a half a mile away, I could see the outline of the house I was building for Nora and myself. It was going to be a close thing to get it finished by our wedding day. Not having any riders to spare for the project, I'd imported a building contractor from Galveston, sixty miles away. He'd arrived with a half a dozen Mexican laborers and a few skilled masons and they'd set up a little tent city around the place. The contractor had gone back to Galveston to fetch more materials, leaving his Mexicans behind. I walked along idly, hoping he wouldn't forget that the job wasn't done. He had some of my money, but not near what he'd get when he finished the job.

Just then Ray Hays came hurrying across the back lot toward me. Ray was kind of a special case for me. The only problem with that was that he knew it and wasn't a bit above taking advantage of the situation. Once, a few years past, he'd saved my life by going against an evil man that he was working for at the time, an evil man who meant to have my life. In gratitude I'd given Ray a good job at the Half-Moon, letting him work directly under Ben, who was responsible for the horse herd. He was a good, steady man and a good man with a gun. He was also fair company. When he wasn't talking.

He came churning up to me, mopping his brow. He said, "Lordy, boss, it is—"

I said, "Hays, if you say it's hot I'm going to knock you down."

He gave me a look that was a mixture of astonishment and hurt. He said, "Why, whatever for?"

I said, "*Everybody* knows it's hot. Does every son of a bitch you run into have to make mention of the fact?"

His brow furrowed. "Well, I never thought of it that way. I 'spect you are right. Goin' down to look at yore house?"

I shook my head. "No. It makes me nervous to see how far they've got to go. I can't see any way it'll be ready on time."

He said, "Miss Nora ain't gonna like that."

I gave him a look. "I guess you felt forced to say that."

He looked down. "Well, maybe she won't mind."

I said, grimly, "The hell she won't. She'll think I did it a-purpose."

"Aw, she wouldn't."

"Naturally you know so much about it, Hays. Why don't you tell me a few other things about her."

"I was jest tryin' to lift yore spirits, boss."

I said, "You keep trying to lift my spirits and I'll put you on the haying crew."

He looked horrified. No real cowhand wanted any work he couldn't do from the back of his horse. Haying was a hot, hard, sweaty job done either afoot or from a wagon seat. We generally brought in contract Mexican labor to handle ours. But I'd been known in the past to discipline a cowhand by giving him a few days on the hay gang. Hays said, "Boss, now I never meant nothin'. I swear. You know me, my mouth gets to runnin' sometimes. I swear I'm gonna watch it."

I smiled. Hays always made me smile. He was so easily buffaloed. He had it soft at the Half-Moon and he knew it and didn't want to take any chances on losing a good thing.

I lit up a cigarillo and watched dusk settle in over the coastal plains. It wasn't but three miles to Matagorda Bay and it was quiet enough I felt like I could almost hear the waves breaking on the shore. Somewhere in the distance a mama cow bawled for her calf. The spring crop were near about weaned by now, but there were still a few mamas that wouldn't cut the apron strings. I stood there reflecting on how peaceful things had been of late. It suited me just fine. All I wanted was to get my house finished, marry Nora and never handle another gun so long as I lived.

The peace and quiet were short-lived. Within twenty-four hours we'd had a return telegram from Jack Cole. It said:

YOUR LAND OCCUPIED BY TEN TO TWELVE MEN STOP CAN'T BE SURE WHAT THEY'RE DOING BECAUSE THEY RUN STRANGERS OFF STOP APPEAR TO HAVE A GOOD MANY CATTLE GATHERED STOP APPEAR TO BE FENCING STOP ALL I KNOW STOP

I read the telegram twice and then I said, "Why this is crazy as hell! That land wouldn't support fifty head of cattle."

We were all gathered in the big office. Even Dad was there, sitting in his rocking chair. I looked up at him. "What do you make of this, Howard?"

He shook his big, old head of white hair. "Beats the hell out of me, Justa. I can't figure it."

Ben said, "Well, I don't see where it has to be figured. I'll take five men and go down there and run them off. I don't care what they're doing. They ain't got no business on our land."

I said, "Take it easy, Ben. Aside from the fact you don't need to be getting into any more fights this year, I can't spare you or five men. The way this grass is drying up we've got to keep drifting those cattle."

Norris said, "No, Ben is right. We can't have such affairs going on with our property. But we'll handle it within the law. I'll simply take the train down there, hire a good lawyer and have the matter settled by the sheriff. Shouldn't take but a few days."

Well, there wasn't much I could say to that. We couldn't very well let people take advantage of us, but I still hated to be without Norris's services even for a few days. On matters other than the ranch he was the expert, and it didn't seem like there was a day went by that some financial question didn't come up that only he could answer. I said, "Are you sure you can spare yourself for a few days?"

He thought for a moment and then nodded. "I don't see why not. I've just moved most of our available cash into short-term municipal bonds in Galveston. The market is looking all right and everything appears fine at the bank. I can't think of anything that might come up."

I said, "All right. But you just keep this in mind. You are not a gun hand. You are not a fighter. I do not want you going anywhere near those people, whoever they are. You do it legal and let the sheriff handle the eviction. Is that understood?"

He kind of swelled up, resenting the implication that he couldn't handle himself. The biggest trouble I'd had through the years when trouble had come up had been keeping Norris out of it. Why he couldn't just be content to be a wagon load of brains was more than I could understand. He said, "Didn't you just hear me say I intended to go through a lawyer and the sheriff? Didn't I just say that?"

I said, "I wanted to be sure you heard yourself."

He said, "Nothing wrong with my hearing. Nor my approach to this matter. You seem to constantly be taken with the idea that I'm always looking for a fight. I think you've got the wrong brother. I use logic."

"Yeah?" I said. "You remember when that guy kicked you in the balls when they were holding guns on us? And then we chased them twenty miles and finally caught them?"

He looked away. "That has nothing to do with this."

"Yeah?" I said, enjoying myself. "And here's this guy, shot all to hell. And what was it you insisted on doing?"

Ben laughed, but Norris wouldn't say anything.

I said, "Didn't you insist on us standing him up so you could kick him in the balls? Didn't you?"

He sort of growled, "Oh, go to hell."

I said, "I just want to know where the logic was in that."

He said, "Right is right. I was simply paying him back in kind. It was the only thing his kind could understand."

I said, "That's my point. You just don't go down there and go to paying back a bunch of rough hombres in kind. Or any other currency for that matter."

That made him look over at Dad. He said, "Dad, will you make him quit treating me like I was ten years old? He does it on purpose."

But he'd appealed to the wrong man. Dad just threw his hands in the air and said, "Don't come to me with your troubles. I'm just a boarder around here. You get your orders from Justa. You know that."

Of course he didn't like that. Norris had always been a strong hand for the right and wrong of a matter. In fact, he may have been one of the most stubborn men I'd ever met. But he didn't say anything, just gave me a look and muttered something about hoping a mess came up at the bank while he was gone and then see how much boss I was.

But he didn't mean nothing by it. Like most families, we fought amongst ourselves and, like most families, God help the outsider who tried to interfere with one of us.

A special offer for people who enjoy reading the best Westerns published today. If you enjoyed this book, subscribe now and get ...

TWO FREE

A $5.90 VALUE—NO OBLIGATION

If you enjoyed this book and would like to read more of the very best Westerns being published today, you'll want to subscribe to True Value's Western Home Subscription Service. If you enjoyed the book you just read and want more of the most exciting, adventurous, action packed Westerns, subscribe now.

Each month the editors of True Value will select the 6 very best Westerns from America's leading publishers for special readers like you. You'll be able to preview these new titles as soon as they are published, FREE for ten days with no obligation.

TWO FREE BOOKS

When you subscribe, we'll send you your first month's shipment of the newest and best 6 Westerns for you to preview. With your first shipment, two of these books will be yours as our introductory gift to you absolutely FREE, regardless of what you decide to do. If you like them, as much as we think you will, keep all six books but pay for just 4 at the low subscriber rate of just $2.45 each. If you decide to return them, keep 2 of the titles as our gift. No obligation.

Special Subscriber Savings

When you become a True Value subscriber you'll save money several ways. First, all regular monthly selections will be billed at the low subscriber price of just $2.45 each. That's

WESTERNS!

at least a savings of $3.00 each month below the publishers price. Second, there is never any shipping, handling or other hidden charges—Free home delivery. What's more there is no minimum number of books you must buy, you may return any selection for full credit and you can cancel your subscription at any time. A TRUE VALUE!

Mail the coupon below

To start your subscription and receive 2 FREE WESTERNS, fill out the coupon below and mail it today. We'll send your first shipment which includes 2 FREE BOOKS as soon as we receive it.